JULIE CALDWELL

ISBN: 979-8-9880180-2-5 (Paperback)

ISBN: 979-8-9880180-3-2 (Ebook)

Book Cover by Miblart

1st edition 2024

To all the people who feel like an outcast, I see you.
Keep being weird.

Also By Julie Caldwell

Of Witches and Ruin

CHAPTER ONE

I ARCED PHANTOMSEEKER, THE Delacroix family sword, at a flying Vastarok—a slimy demon with no eyes and talons on their wings. My sword sliced clean through the flesh and bone of the demon, raining thick black blood all over me. I tried not to gag as the vile substance entered my mouth. I spit as much of it out as I could, but I was definitely going to use mouthwash when I got home.

It's been six months since my distant cousin, Fabian Delacroix, decided to destroy both the human world and my home world of Amethystia.

It hadn't gone well.

Demons had been running amok in both realms and my family and I had been trying to beat them back with no luck, and no permanent solution in sight. Some witches who had hated my family since they came into power heard about me killing Fabian and decided to rebel. They've been helping the witch hunters—well, hunt witches.

"Ebony!"

I whirled around, my hair sticking to my face as I watched my boyfriend, Nightshade Oakenheart, rush toward me. His pointed ears showed through his long lavender hair. I sheathed my sword as he reached for me.

"Are you alright?" He grabbed my waist and slid his light purple eyes over me, scanning for injuries.

My breath hitched, his familiar scent of vanilla and musk overpowering the smell of the blood. He smirked and his hands roved up my torso, slowly lifting my tank top, as he looked into my eyes.

"Ahem."

Nightshade and I jerked away from each other as Aunt Jasmine peered at us with her hands on her hips.

"Would you two please save that kind of thing for home?"

We nodded sheepishly, and my face heated as I adjusted my shirt.

The three of us dragged our feet as we headed back to the house to get cleaned up. About halfway there, we heard a high-pitched scream and immediately went on alert.

The scream sounded again, and before I could think about what kind of nasty creature I was about to encounter, my feet were in motion. Nightshade called after me, but I didn't slow down. Someone was in trouble, and I needed to help.

I ran through the street and didn't stop until I was in front of the high school. Nightshade was right behind me and pulled me back as I started toward the door that would lead to the gym.

"I don't get it," I said. "Where's the demon?"

Nightshade wouldn't meet my eyes, and he started chewing on his lip.

"What's going on?"

Nightshade shifted from one foot to the other. "Lady Jasmine and I did not want to tell you. We did not want you to do anything rash."

I put my hands on my hips. "What are you talking about?"

Before he could answer, Nightshade grabbed me by the elbow and hauled me behind a bush. A few seconds later, a group of people came out of the gym entrance and headed into the forest. In front of the group was a girl that looked about my age with her blonde hair in pigtails and next to her... my heart stopped. Next to her was a boy with caramel colored hair, and a face that had once been friendly but now bore a sneer.

Sam.

I hadn't seen him since the funeral of our other friend, Melissa McFadden and we didn't leave things on the best of terms. In fact, the last time we spoke, he said he would kill me if I used magic again.

I still had nightmares about Melissa's death. Fabian's hand wrapped around her throat, the smell of burning flesh as he electrocuted her with magic, the sound of her body thumping against the hard ground.

I tried to get up, but Nightshade held me in place.

"What are you doing?" I snapped. "I have to go after him."

Nightshade bit his bottom lip and motioned for me to follow him. Together, we trailed behind Sam and the others, the screaming getting louder. A clearing appeared about a hundred yards in front of us and we ducked behind a large fallen log, close enough to see what was going on, but far enough away where we wouldn't be spotted.

I saw a medium-sized crowd gathered around an erect piece of wood. Tied to the pole was a young girl, no more than twelve. Tears were streaming down her face as she struggled against the bonds that held her. Her screams filled the air and hurt my ears. I watched in horror as Sam and the girl went to the front of the crowd and hushed the people.

"You all know why we're here," the girl said, "We need to cleanse this world of the filth that has taken root."

The crowd cheered, and the girl raised her arms in the air to silence them. She turned to Sam and handed him something I couldn't see.

"Sweetheart, would you care to do the honors?"

Sweetheart? Sam whirled toward the girl and flicked open a lighter.

No.

Nightshade gripped my shoulder as I struggled. Sam tossed the lighter at the girl tied to the wooden pole and flames whooshed up in a column so large I thought someone could have viewed it from space. The girl screamed louder than I thought possible as the fire engulfed her. I buried my face in Nightshade's shoulder, sobbing. He stroked his hand down my back in a soothing gesture. I looked back when the screams died and saw the crowd drinking and laughing. They just killed a child. An innocent child and they were having a party to celebrate?

"She was innocent." I whispered, my voice so far away I wasn't sure it came from me.

"She was a witch."

Nightshade and I whirled around to find Sam leaning casually against a tree.

"What have you done?" I asked.

Sam shrugged as he inspected his nails. "I did what I told you I was going to do."

"Which is what, exactly?" I sunk into Nightshade, who was looking at Sam with sadness in his eyes.

Nightshade bit his bottom lip, trying to decide whether to tell me. He decided not to. I rolled my eyes, but his scent wrapped around me and calmed me. I snuggled into him and he rested his cheek on top of my head.

"I love you," he whispered into my hair.

"I love you too." I closed my eyes and fell asleep in his arms, dreaming about those little girl's screams.

CHAPTER TWO

I AWOKE THE NEXT morning with bleary eyes, having tossed and turned the entire night. At one point, I actually kicked Nightshade onto the floor, where he stayed for the rest of the night, not wanting me to hurt him again.

I dressed in a tank top and jeans and meandered downstairs to get the darkest coffee I could find. With Presto Espresso out of business thanks to a rather nasty demon attack that left the building in rubble, home brew was all I got.

"Ebony, come here please," Aunt Jasmine called from the living room.

I groaned but made my way into the living room where Aunt Jasmine, Nightshade and one of my uncle's advisors stood. Nightshade looked just as bleary as I did, his light purple eyes drooping as he stood at attention.

"Hello, Princess." The advisor bowed at the waist.

I gave an awkward wave and flopped onto the couch, waiting for an explanation of why he was here.

"Your uncle sent for you. He has... some things he wishes to discuss."

I let my head fall back. "Can't he send a shimmer message like a normal person?"

The advisor shuffled from one foot to the other. "He's afraid of someone intercepting the message. He said to tell you it's an emergency. We should really go now."

I stood up and Nightshade followed the movement. He wasn't my boyfriend right now. He was my bodyguard, and that difference made me take my uncle's advisor seriously.

"Let's go," I said.

The advisor opened a portal as Nightshade held out his hand. I grabbed it, relishing the feeling of his warmth, and together we walked through to Amethystia.

The throne room looked just as I remembered it at first glance, with hundreds of burning candles warming the worn cobblestones and making the purple ivy that clung to the wall glow in an ethereal light, but something felt different. I peered around the room and noticed several sigils on the wall for protection and warding and then I noticed large gashes in the stone.

Claw marks.

Uncle Hesperus was sitting on his throne looking as regal as ever, but with a tired edge. He had his long, dark brown hair tied back and his signature white streak was caked with dirt. His eyes were weary as he talked to my dad, who was standing beside him with what looked like a folder tucked under his arm.

There was a boy with shaggy brown hair lounging in the chair opposite them, cleaning his nails with a dagger. He looked to be around my age, maybe a couple of years older. I rolled my eyes. The air around him screamed arrogance. I ignored him as I strolled up to my uncle's throne. Dad and Uncle Hesperus stopped talking as I approached, and they smiled at me. I smiled back as I stepped onto the dais that my uncle's throne sat on and wrapped my arms around him. I stepped out of his embrace and hugged my dad. He squeezed me back, but stiffened as Nightshade came to my side. I let out a small sigh as I let go and wrapped my arm around Nightshade's waist. My dad was never a fan of Nightshade and me being together. He thought it would look bad to the people, but to his credit, he's stopped being vocal about it.

"Hey guys," I said, "I like what you've done with the place."

Dad narrowed his eyes, and Uncle Hesperus sighed, his tired eyes drooping even more.

"A cluster of demons attacked the palace. We don't know how they got in, but we lost several servants, and a couple of my advisors."

I whirled toward Dad. "Mom?"

"She's okay. Don't worry, she's upstairs," Dad said.

I sagged with relief, but my body stiffened as I felt an arrogant presence by my side.

"As much fun as this little family reunion is, you summoned me here because you guys had something of a problem, and I would like to know what it is."

Uncle Hesperus cleared his throat. "Right. Ebony, Nightshade, this is Peyton Levin. He's a—"

"A very impatient person, so can we get this show on the road?"

Peyton's dagger glinted in his hand as Nightshade tightened his arm around me.

Uncle Hesperus merely raised an eyebrow at him for the interruption, but moved on.

"The people of Amethystia have been restless, and with demons roaming the streets, they have grown fearful. They're now turning that fear on each other. And us."

"'Us' meaning the royal family?" I asked.

"Give the girl a medal," Peyton mumbled.

I sneered at him, and Nightshade squeezed my waist.

I wiggled out of his grasp and pointed my finger in Peyton's face. "Just who are you, anyway?"

He just shrugged and started cleaning his nails again.

I turned back to my uncle. "What do you need me to do?"

Uncle Hesperus rose stiffly from the throne, and he walked with a limp. "There's a protest outside the gates right now. I need you to quell the panic. Nightshade and Peyton will be there to make sure things don't get out of hand."

"And if things go south?"

Uncle Hesperus glanced at Nightshade and then at Peyton. "Then your bodyguards will get you out."

Nightshade nodded once while Peyton rolled his eyes.

"Be careful," Dad said. "These people are scared, and fear may make them do deranged things."

With that, Peyton, Nightshade, and I walked out of the throne room and into chaos.

Chaos might have been a bit of an understatement. I heard the yelling before we had even walked into the courtyard, and once outside, I resisted the urge to cover my ears. The noise was deafening.

Luckily, the wrought-iron gates were closed, so we weren't in any immediate danger, but people threw rotten food between the bars and the smell was sickly sweet in the spring heat. Uncle Hesperus had stationed guards on either side of the gates, keeping the crowd at bay, but they were struggling. I squared my shoulders and walked toward the gates with Peyton and Nightshade flanking me. The screams became more heated as the people noticed me, and I wanted to shrink back into the comfort of Nightshade's arms. But I was part of the royal family, and I couldn't show weakness.

I stopped a few feet away from the gate and cleared my throat. Speaking in a clear, loud voice, I addressed the crowd.

"People of Amethystia, my name is Ebony Amberwood. Some of you may know me as the exiled princess, and some of you may know me as the person who saved this realm. I understand your pain and I know you're scared, but please believe me when I say you are safe. My family is doing everything we can to beat back the demons that Fabian Delacroix unleashed on this world. We will get rid of them and we will restore peace."

"You're the one we need to be saved from, Ebony."

My heart stopped. I knew that voice. That was the voice of my nightmares. Evan Felder, my ex-boyfriend, made his way to the front of the crowd and gripped the iron bars as if to bend them apart and step through. He had his jet-black hair styled in a way that made it look like he had put no effort into it, and his dark brown eyes shone with hate. His biceps strained against the fabric of his long-sleeved shirt, making him look every bit as strong as I remembered. I hated him. I put my hands on my hips and put as much attitude as possible into my next words.

"I'm surprised to see you aren't in prison... considering everything you've done."

Evan's lips turned up in a cruel smile. "Remember, *Princess*, you did those things with me. And you enjoyed them just as much as I did."

"I don't know what you're talking about Evan, and what do you mean by I'm the one people need saving from?"

Evan crossed his arms. "You know exactly what I'm talking about. You're the one who opened that portal and nearly destroyed us, and don't deny it.

Just because your crooked family rules this realm, don't think that will protect you."

My hands slackened at my sides. I was dumbfounded. There was no way people could think that I—

Chants filled the air, booing me, and some people even threw some of the rotten food at my head. Nightshade and Peyton stepped closer to me, but I signaled for them to stay back.

"Lies won't make you any more of a hero, Evan. Eventually, these people will remember what kind of person you are, and when they do, I'll be there with a big bag of popcorn."

Evan's smile grew, like he was expecting me to say that. "Oh, but do these people know who *you* are?" His voice rose, carrying to the back of the mob. "Do they know you are a Delacroix? Are they aware of your relationship with Fabian? How do we know you and your cousin weren't in this together?"

My mouth went slack. "H-how do you know that?"

Evan grabbed the bars once more and leaned in close. "I know a lot about you, Ebony. Things you wouldn't even dream of."

Evan leaned back and gave me a lazy smile as the crowd's cries grew. Nightshade stiffened. He grabbed my arm, and I let him pull me back toward the safety of the palace. The rotten food that was being thrown randomly was now being aimed directly at me as the crowd grew more restless. The guards shifted as if they were ready to throw themselves into the fray if things got out of hand. Nightshade marched at my side and Peyton meandered behind us as we went back inside.

Nightshade and Peyton reported to the throne room to fill Uncle Hesperus in on what occurred. When they were gone, I sank to the floor of the foyer and hugged my knees to my chest. Tears threatened to fall. Who did Evan think he was? And how did he know about my heritage? Someone sat down beside me and I looked up to find my mother staring at me. She had her long platinum blonde hair braided down her back and her light blue eyes, which were so much like mine, shone with pride.

"I heard everything. You did well," she said.

I scoffed. "Tell that to the enraged crowd outside."

Mom put her arm around my shoulders. "That was because of Evan. Don't let him get the best of you. He hasn't done half the things you have, and he knows it makes him inferior."

"I didn't do anything. The demons got through the portal, and I couldn't stop them. Fabian destroyed both worlds, and my only job was to keep him from doing that, and then the crowd outside pelted me with rotten fruit because I couldn't ease their fear." I pulled a piece of tomato from my hair.

Mom lifted my chin and forced me to look her in the eye. "Ebony Amberwood, if it weren't for you, all of us would be dead."

My eyes fell as she said that. "Some of us are."

Mom held me to her and smoothed my hair down. "Melissa would have been so proud of you, you know."

I pulled away from her. "You didn't know her."

"But I know you, and I know people gravitate toward you. Even if you try to push them away."

I gave a half smile and stood up. "I must be doing something right then."

Mom stood up a second later and kissed the top of my head. "Yes, you must be."

CHAPTER THREE

NIGHTSHADE AND I SPENT the next few days in Amethystia. We both agreed we couldn't leave the rioting crowd unchecked. Peyton, to my surprise, was also staying at the palace for a few days. I rolled my eyes when he told me that, and he just gave me a wink and walked away. Nightshade wasn't happy about the news either, and we made moves to avoid interacting with him at all costs. Of course, that backfired almost immediately when one of the servants sent word we would eat dinner with him and the family that evening. I huffed as I flopped onto my bed and stared at the crystal chandelier making rainbows in the middle of the room.

"We could always say we are dealing with the commotion outside," Nightshade suggested.

I shook my head. "Uncle Hesperus would never believe that. Neither would my mom or dad. They saw how we were with Peyton."

Nightshade lay down next to me and wrapped his arms around my waist. The familiar scent of vanilla and musk washed over me. I snuggled closer to him and he laid his cheek on top of my head. We stayed like that until the dinner bell rang. We begrudgingly made our way to the dining hall, where Peyton was sitting with his feet on the table.

I avoided the urge to clench my teeth and sat down as far away from him as I could. Nightshade took a seat to my left, between me and Peyton, and Peyton smirked.

Seconds later, someone ushered Mom and Dad into the room. Peyton took his feet off the table immediately. Uncle Hesperus entered the room soon after and the awkward silence seemed to dissipate. For the time being.

Dinner was silent for the most part, with Mom and Dad asking me the occasional question about my life and how things were going in Salem. Nightshade kept glancing at Peyton, and Peyton kept smirking at him. What was their deal? After dinner, I took Nightshade's hand and led him to my favorite place.

The underground garden smelled of roses, jasmine, and lavender. Once, when she was here with me, Melissa had asked me how the flowers grew underground, and I explained the glowing crystals littering the ceiling gave off the energy needed for the flowers to grow. Nightshade stared at me as I stared at those crystals. He gently took my hand and squeezed it, but I found it less comforting and more annoying. Like he knew what I was thinking about and was trying to shield me from the fact that Melissa was no longer here. Like Sam hadn't threatened my life six months ago over her death and then ran off with a bunch of witch hunters and is now burning innocents at the stake.

I jerked my hand away, needing to think about anything else. Casting a quick glance at the shimmering pool of water, I flashed Nightshade a mischievous grin. I ran toward it, shedding my clothes as I went. Nightshade called after me, his voice echoing in the large chamber, but I ignored him and cannonballed into the cold, sparkling water. My head broke the surface, and I beckoned to Nightshade.

"Come on in. The water feels great."

Nightshade's face was red, making his dark tan deeper, but his expression was one of disapproval. "Ebony, what are you doing? Come on out of there. Someone will see you."

I twirled around in the water, laughing, trying to get him to come join me, but Nightshade wouldn't budge from where he was standing.

"You're such a buzzkill," I said. "Come on, skinny-dipping won't hurt you."

He shook his head and crossed his arms. I pouted, but swam around some more. I dived back underwater, and when I surfaced again, I splashed Nightshade right in the face.

"Ebony, cut it out. I am serious. Get out of the pool."

My mood darkened. He was serious. To him, I must have been acting like a child that needed to be disciplined. Tears welled up behind my eyes as I climbed out of the water. I didn't look at Nightshade as he shrugged off his jacket and wrapped it around me. I couldn't hold back the tears, and Nightshade wrapped me in a comforting hug, but I shrugged out of his embrace. He looked wounded, his eyes clouded, and he bit his bottom lip, but he stayed at my side. We were walking out of the garden just as Peyton was walking in. He stopped short when he saw me, wet and crying, and his face turned from nonchalant to downright hostile, but there was something odd in his eyes that I couldn't quite place.

"Did you push her in?" His voice was eerily calm. When Nightshade didn't answer him, he pushed Nightshade away from me and tried to punch him in the face. Nightshade dodged the strike perfectly, but didn't dodge the sweeping kick to his ankle that made him fall flat on the ground. Peyton was on top of Nightshade in an instant, getting ready to throw another punch.

"Stop!" I sobbed.

"I did not push her in," Nightshade said calmly. "She threw off her clothes and jumped in. I got her out."

Peyton paused at the explanation and looked at my clothes, still on the ground, and then back to Nightshade. Then Peyton did something unexpected. He laughed. It was more like a cackle, but he got off Nightshade and held out his hand to help him up. Nightshade refused the help and stalked past the both of us. I reached out to him, but he shrugged me off. I stared after him, dumbfounded, my wet hair sticking to me and making me shiver even through Nightshade's coat. Peyton swaggered over to me.

He leaned down and whispered in my ear, "If you still want to go skinny dipping, I'll do it with you."

I turned around and shoved him away, tears coming down in droves. "Why did you do that? Why did you have to ruin everything?"

Peyton raised an eyebrow. "Your impulsive nature ruined whatever you two were doing down here."

I stomped my foot in frustration and yelled. He was getting on my last nerve. I whirled away from him, grabbed my clothes from the ground, and started stomping off toward my room to get dry, but Peyton caught my arm.

"If you want to go through the castle with no clothes on, be my guest, but if you want to make it upstairs with no one noticing you, follow me."

He let my arm go and led me to an alcove in the back of the garden that was nearly invisible if you didn't know how to spot it. The alcove led to a set of spiral stone stairs that seemed to go on forever.

"It goes all the way to the top of the palace," Peyton explained. "We'll need some light to see, though."

I held out my hand, palm up, and whispered, "*Illuminare.*"

A ball of glowing light appeared above our heads and illuminated the stairwell.

"How have I never noticed this was here? I come down here all the time," I said.

Peyton grabbed my hand and together we ascended the staircase. "Because you are oblivious."

"You don't even know me, so how could you possibly know that?"

Peyton shrugged and just continued to lead me up the stairs. We reached the top and a closed door stood tall in front of us. Peyton motioned for me to open it. My hands pressed against the cool, rough wood and pushed. The door opened into the hallway next to my room. We stepped through the doorway, and I extinguished the light. I turned back, but the door had disappeared.

"How—"

"I told you. You can be oblivious." Peyton strode in front of me and opened the door to my room. He stepped aside to let me in.

"Your room awaits, Your Highness. And next time you want to get naked with a guy, call me. I'm always available."

He left me in the middle of the room, staring after him.

After changing into some fluffy pajamas, I headed into the sitting room and wrote Aunt Jasmine a shimmer message telling her I was coming home soon. I didn't know if Nightshade would come back home with me or not after tonight's events, though. I thought back to the look on his face. He had been so disappointed in me. Like a parent with an unruly child. Tears threatened to fall again, and I pushed them back as I heard a knock. I opened the door to my mother, in her nightgown, smiling faintly at me.

"Bad date with Nightshade?" she asked.

I opened the door wider, letting her in. "You could say that."

She plopped herself down on my bed and waved a servant in. They had a tray with bowls of fruit and sugar, and Mom popped a strawberry into her mouth while motioning for me to join her. I stared at her for a moment, but settled myself on the bed next to her.

"Boys can be... confusing at the best of times," Mom started, "but you have to learn how to navigate them just like they have to learn how to navigate us."

I ate a piece of melon. "How do I do that?"

She smiled. "Be direct with him. Tell him how you're feeling about everything."

"I tell him I love him all the time," I said.

Mom shook her head. "Jasmine told me you haven't really talked about what happened all those months ago. It's not good to keep it all bottled up. It will eat you alive."

My mood instantly went from depressed to guarded. Where was she headed with this?

"What are you saying?" I asked.

She put her hand on my knee. "I'm saying if you won't talk to your family about what happened, at least talk to Nightshade. He loves you and he wants to be there to help you."

I thought about what she was asking me to do. She was right. I shut down whenever I think about what happened. Could I actually talk to someone about it? Would Nightshade understand that it's all my fault that Melissa died? Or would he look at me with disgust? Hell, I looked at myself with disgust. Before I could answer Mom, someone threw a rock through my window, and we both jumped.

I got off the bed and picked up the rock. There was a note attached to it. I untied the string and unfolded the note.

Surprise

Before I could react, Mom cried out. I spun and saw a flash of caramel colored hair before everything went black.

CHAPTER FOUR

I WOKE UP TO the smell of gasoline. I examined my surroundings, and vaguely recognized where I was, only it wasn't the same as I remembered. The wooden floor of the high school gym was torn up and broken windows were everywhere. I was back in the human world, but I didn't understand how. Muffled cries came from my right, and when I turned toward the sound, I screamed. Or tried to. Just like my mother beside me, someone had tied me to a stake and wrapped a cloth tightly around my mouth, keeping me from making much noise.

"Scream all you want, Ebony, it won't do you any good."

I looked around for the source of the voice and found, standing in front of me, the same blonde-haired girl in pigtails who burned that little girl. I struggled, but my hands were bound by a rope behind me and the more I moved, the more it hurt. Sam strolled up beside her, put his arm around her waist, and kissed her cheek. If I wasn't gagged, I might have hurled.

Sam walked up to me and took off the gag. "Don't struggle, Ebony. It will only make this worse."

"What are you doing, Sam? Let us go. We won't hurt you."

Sam shook his head. "But you already have. You took everything from me, Ebony. You *and* your family. The only way you'll ever learn your lesson is if I take everything from you."

I struggled more, the rope biting into my wrists. "What are you talking about? What do you mean, take everything from me?"

Sam pulled out a lighter, and Mom screamed beside me.

"What are you going to do, Sam?" I asked, "Kill us? You're not a murderer."

"No, but you are." He flicked the lighter open and closed several times. "Tell me something. Did you even try to save her from being electrocuted by your demented cousin? Or were you too busy making out with him to notice?"

"That was one time!" The rope bit into my wrists more, breaking skin. The warmth of blood trickled down my hands.

Same paced in front of me. "Twice actually, if I remember right." He stopped in front of my mother and flicked the lighter open once more.

The pigtailed girl bounced up to Sam and put her hand on his shoulder. "Let's just be done with this, baby."

"Who the hell are you, anyway?" I demanded.

She didn't even look in my direction when she said, "My name is Delilah. Delilah Larkin. My father used to be one of the biggest contributors to this town, and you witches killed him." She stroked Sam's hair, and he closed his eyes. "Now, we're killing you. Isn't that right, baby?"

Sam opened his eyes, and they had a new determination in them. He glanced at me as he threw the lighter down at his feet. Flames erupted and went straight for my mother.

"Sam!" I struggled against my bonds, but it was no use. They were too tight.

"Sam, please no! Please!"

I whipped my head to the right when a blood-curdling scream filled the air. The kindling surrounding my mother's feet caught fire and flames climbed up her body. Sam and Delilah walked away as my mother's screams continued. Tears flowed freely as I screamed for help over and over, watching my mother burn. Her screams abruptly stopped, but I kept screaming for someone, anyone, to help.

My voice went hoarse long before I stopped yelling. The tears wouldn't stop. The smell of burnt flesh wafted through the air, filling my nostrils with its sweet, putrid scent. I dared a glance at my mother. Her flesh was burnt to a crisp and black stained bone shone through her charred skin. Her jaw was agape in terror and her eyes had melted. I vomited all over the ground. And myself.

I heard light footsteps sprinting through the halls and Nightshade burst through the gym doors. He stopped dead when he saw the scene before him.

"Nightshade," I croaked. "My mom... she needs help... please... help her."

He rushed to me and untied my arms. I slumped onto my knees as Nightshade held me. I protested at his grip. My mom still needed help. She needed...

A fresh wave of sobs broke through my chest and I screamed some more as his scent of vanilla and musk masked the smell of my mother's charred flesh. He tightened his hold on me as he soothed my hair down and made calming noises. My entire body shook and lights danced across my eyes. I knew what they meant, and I dug my nails into Nightshade's arms as the vision overtook me.

I stood in a large cave, the air around me clean and earthy, driving away the horror of my surroundings back in reality. The sound of water dripping echoed through the space. A stone well stood before me, moss growing up the sides. A glowing golden pentagram with symbols that swirled around it covered the opening, illuminating the cave. In the middle of the pentagram was an open eye, staring into my soul. The eye blinked, and I backed up.

"Ebony," someone said from behind me.

I spun around and faced the person who spoke and gasped. She shouldn't have been there. She couldn't have been there. Melissa was dead. She looked the same though, with her golden blonde hair in perfect curls and her deep blue eyes that were as clear as the ocean. My vision blurred with more tears.

"I'm sorry," I said.

"You have nothing to be sorry for, but you have to listen to me." She walked over to me. "Delilah is not who she seems. She's working with others—"

"Yeah, Sam, I know. He..." I couldn't finish the rest of that sentence, because my mother...

"No." Melissa shook her head. "Sam is only a pawn. Save him. Don't let him go down this path, Ebony. He needs you."

"It's too late. He's already gone."

My eyes cast downward. I couldn't bear to tell Melissa what he's done.

She wrapped me in a big hug. "It's never too late for anyone to be saved. And don't trust the man who created this place. He's bad news."

"Who?"

Melissa broke the hug, and tears glistened in her deep blue eyes. "It doesn't matter, but remember this place. It's important."

The pentagram emitted a pulsing light, and when the light died, Melissa was gone.

I gasped as I came back to reality. I released Nightshade's arms and saw that I had broken skin with my nails.

"What did you see?" he asked.

"I saw Melissa." Tears rolled down my cheeks again as I tried to remember the details of her face.

Nightshade held my shoulders as he looked into my eyes.

"I think you are in shock. Visions do not come in the form of the dead."

I shook him off and shakily got to my feet. "I know what I saw."

Nightshade stood, and his face told me he didn't believe me. That was fine. He didn't have to. I knew it was Melissa.

The crackling of the embers turned my attention back to my mother. The fire had died down, and all it left was a carcass. I took a deep, shaky breath and tamped down the tears that threatened to overtake me once more.

"Let's go home. I need to talk to Aunt Jasmine. And... and tell my dad that Mom... that she... about what happened."

Aunt Jasmine's house was a flurry of movement when we stepped inside the entryway. Guards were stomping all over the clean carpet, leaving boot prints in their wake. Dad, Uncle Hesperus, and Aunt Jasmine huddled over the table in the living room. Uncle Hesperus was using his scrying mirror. I cleared my too hoarse throat, and all movement stopped. Nightshade put his hand on the small of my back and led me to my awaiting family. I didn't even feel it when Dad pulled me into his arms. Nightshade excused himself to go talk to the captain of the guard, who was standing just out of earshot. I wiggled my way out of Dad's grasp and cast my eyes down. I knew I needed to tell them, but I couldn't. Not when... not when it was my fault my mom died. Just like it was my fault Melissa died. My memories went back to the mean girl at my school, Richelle. She had been a witch hunter working with Fabian to kill us all and it had ended with a battle and ultimately, her death. I was the one who had killed her. I was responsible for so many deaths. My knees wobbled, and I fell to the ground, unable to hold my own weight. Sobs overtook my body, and Aunt Jasmine knelt beside me, looking frantic.

The captain of the guard motioned Uncle Hesperus and my dad over and said something to them while Aunt Jasmine and I just sat on the dirty carpet as I cried. A loud bang sounded and broke me out of my sob fest long enough to see that the sound was Dad's fist going through the drywall. His eyes glistened. I had never seen my father cry before, but silent tears fell and I knew what the captain told him. What I did and what I couldn't say. Aunt Jasmine got off the floor and went over to my dad. Uncle Hesperus took her place on the ground, and he gently put his hand on my shoulder.

"Ebony, we need to know what happened. Who did this?"

I shook my head. I couldn't say it. Couldn't even think about it.

"Was... was it Sam who did this, Ebony?" Uncle Hesperus's voice was softer than I had ever heard it, and it made the sobs start again.

I shook my head. I did this. Sam had only pulled the trigger or flicked the lighter in this case. Uncle Hesperus pulled me close. He helped me up and ordered someone to take me to my room. A callused hand grabbed my arm gently, and I let them lead me upstairs.

They sat me down on the bed and wrapped a blanket around me. I shrugged it off. They just sighed and wrapped it back around me.

"You're in shock. Trust me, you'll need the blanket," he said.

I finally looked at who brought me up here. Peyton's ice-blue eyes met mine as he stood in front of me, no trace of the arrogance that usually stained his features. His face was solemn, but his eyes held icy rage just beneath the surface.

"I don't want a blanket," I croaked. "It's too hot."

"Then why are you shivering?"

I gave him a solitary finger, and he smirked. "There she is. I knew you wouldn't stay down long."

I wiped my soot covered face, but it did nothing for the feeling of disgust rolling over me. I stood up and dropped the blanket.

"I want a shower." My voice sounded so far away that I wasn't sure if it was mine.

Peyton nodded and followed me as I went down the hall to the bathroom. He stationed himself outside the door as I clicked the lock and slowly started peeling my clothes off. My shirt was full of burn holes and the front of it was covered in vomit. I threw it in the trash and turned on the shower. As soon as the water hit me, so did another wave of sobs. I didn't know how long I stayed in the shower, but the tears dried up long before I turned off the water.

When I finally deemed myself decent enough to face the world again, I wrapped a towel around my body and readied myself for Peyton's commentary. When I opened the door, however, I found Nightshade on the other side.

"I thought you might want a more familiar face with you tonight," he said.

I gave a half smile and nodded as he followed me to my room. Nightshade turned away as I got into pj's, and he tucked me into bed. I noticed a chair that hadn't been in the room when I left and gave Nightshade a questioning look.

"I do not think it is wise for me to be in bed with you tonight."

I snorted. "Because you aren't my boyfriend tonight, right? Tonight, you are my faithful bodyguard."

"Why do you say that?" he asked.

I gave him a sharp look. "Don't think I don't notice that you never get close to me whenever you're in bodyguard mode. Why can't you be my bodyguard *and* my boyfriend tonight?"

Hurt shone on Nightshade's face. "Because when I am close to you, I cannot think about anything else but you. Your scent, the way your skin feels on mine. I love you, Ebony and I will not put you in danger because of it."

"I'm sorry. I'm just not feeling like myself lately. Actually, I haven't felt like myself since that night."

Nightshade sat down on the edge of my bed and put his hand on my knee. The warmth of his skin felt nice, and it gave me the courage to tell him what I hadn't been able to say.

"The battle with Fabian. It was unlike anything I ever had to do before, and I can't get it out of my head."

Nightshade's hand tightened on my knee. "Cannot get what exactly out of your head?"

"Any of it. The Jaramoths cornering us, finding out I'm a Delacroix, and especially Melissa's death."

Nightshade leaned in and pressed his lips to my temple in a comforting gesture. I leaned into that touch, and his breath tickled my face as he sighed.

"Get some sleep, my love."

I nodded and lay down as Nightshade took his place in the chair. Even though he was right beside me, I hugged myself as the empty space in my bed left me cold and alone.

CHAPTER FIVE

NIGHTSHADE SHOOK ME AWAKE. It was still dark out, and a sheen of sweat coated my skin. He smoothed my hair and tried to calm me down as a bead of sweat trickled down the back of my neck. The air was too thick. I tried to gulp down a breath, but couldn't. My throat was tight and my mouth felt like a desert. Nightshade rubbed soothing circles on my back and breathing became easier.

"You are all right," he promised.

"What happened?" I asked.

"You were screaming. What were you dreaming about?"

"Fire. I heard Mom screaming. The flames were so hot." I gasped.

Peyton burst into the room with his dagger drawn. He had nothing on but a pair of pants, his muscular chest almost shining in the moonlight from my window. Nightshade huffed and stood between me and Peyton.

"We are fine. You can go."

Peyton sized Nightshade up and then turned his attention to me. "Are you okay?"

I nodded. Something in my expression must have been off, though, because Peyton pushed past Nightshade and came to sit by me. He gave me a once over and smirked.

"You look like Death's chew toy."

"Oh, really? Looking at your face, I would have thought that was your job."

Peyton laughed, and I heard the door slam. I looked over and Nightshade was gone.

Peyton's face was smug. "Look's like your little boy toy can't handle some competition."

I stilled. "There is no competition. It will always be Nightshade. I love him and he loves me."

Peyton gave me a side-eyed glance. "Is there a reason he's jealous, then?"

I rolled over and dutifully ignored him.

Peyton chuckled and left. I should have fallen asleep thinking about Nightshade, but a bare-chested brunette with icy blue eyes invaded my thoughts as unconsciousness took me.

The earthy scent of the bright green moss met my nostrils as I stood in front of the well from my vision. The symbols covering the well seemed to glow brighter as I peered at them. Like words that were trying to enter my mind.

"Ebony."

I whirled around and saw my mother. I jogged toward her, but the more I ran, the farther away she seemed to get.

"Mom, wh-where are we? What's going on?"

Her figure shimmered, like a mirage. "I'm sorry honey, you have to figure that out on your own. I'm only here to tell you that you need to find this place, and soon."

I took a step toward her. She didn't move. "I'm sorry I couldn't save you."

"But you will save everyone else. I have faith in you. Now go. We have limited time together. Tell your father the Seal is real."

The cave filled with a bright golden light, and my eyes opened to my bedroom, sunlight pouring through my window. I sighed. I hated prophetic dreams.

I trudged downstairs and found the living room empty. No guards milling about, no Aunt Jasmine painting, no one. I went to the kitchen and put on a pot of coffee before making my way out to the deck. Nightshade wasn't outside meditating like he did every morning. There was no one in the entire house. I went out the front door and noticed why everyone seemed to be missing.

Peyton, my dad, Aunt Jasmine, Uncle Hesperus, Nightshade and the captain of the guard all stood on the front lawn facing a group of humans who held crosses and signs painted with various insults. Sam wasn't among them, but that didn't mean they weren't a part of his witch hunting militia. One human had an unlit torch in his hand, and another had a rope hanging at their side. There was one man who stood slightly in front of the rest of the group. I marched up to him and faced the crowd.

"What's going on here?" I asked.

Nightshade pulled on my arm to drag me back, but I shook him off.

"Are you a witch too, then?" the man in front asked.

"I might be. I might not be. Who wants to know?" I crossed my arms.

The man smirked. "Name's Harlow, and you are going to leave this town. Now."

"And if we don't?" Aunt Jasmine challenged.

Harlow's eyes slid to hers. "Well, you're getting out of here one way or the other. Either you leave peacefully, or we tie you up like dogs and force you out."

"This has been my home for years. You will not force me to leave just because you don't like what we are," she said.

Harlow looked at the rest of our group and then at me. His face became solemn.

"Look, we heard about what that other group did to you and that other one. We aren't like them. I don't intend to kill you, but you all have to go."

Peyton walked forward and stood next to me. "What if there were a way for all of us to live peacefully?"

Harlow looked at his group and then back at us. "I'm listening."

"There is a well in our world that is said to be the source of all magic. If we can somehow drain the well, magic will be gone. Forever. And every witch will be normal. Human." Peyton unsheathed the dagger he always kept on him and started cleaning his nails while he waited for Harlow's response.

"How will that take care of the monsters?" Harlow asked.

Peyton shrugged. "Demons are magical creatures. If we end magic, that means we end *all* magic."

"Let them try, Daddy." A girl stepped forward from the crowd.

She couldn't have been more than fifteen, but that wasn't what struck me. She looked almost identical to Melissa and for a brief minute, my breathing stopped. This girl's features were sharper than Melissa's, with angled cheekbones and a sharp chin. Her hair was just as curly, although this girl had more of an ash tone to her blonde hair, while Melissa's had been golden. Her blue eyes were just as striking, with the same friendliness in them that Melissa had.

"I don't know, Valerie..." Harlow hesitated.

"Mom would have wanted you to."

That sentence seemed to sway him. Harlow turned back toward us and nodded once. Peyton put his dagger away and nodded back.

"Now wait a minute." The captain of the guard stalked forward. "This boy has no right to speak for us, so we will certainly not be entertaining—"

"I'll allow it." Uncle Hesperus said.

I had almost forgotten we had an audience behind us, but Uncle Hesperus came forward and motioned for his captain to retreat, which he did. Uncle Hesperus held out his hand to Harlow, who shook it reluctantly.

"My name is Hesperus Amberwood. I rule the magical realm in which we reside. We have been working on a way of getting rid of the demons permanently and if this is the best option for that, I will send my guards to find this well."

Harlow pursed his lips, weighing my uncle's words. Then he turned around and motioned for the crowd to disperse.

"I want to go with them, Daddy." Valerie said.

Harlow placed his hand on the girl's shoulders and squeezed. "I know you want to help, but I think you would only be in their way. Besides, I'm not losing you in a magical world where we don't know what the dangers are."

Valerie's face fell. I knew what it was like to feel powerless and I felt sorry for the girl, but Harlow was right. Amethystia was no place for a human.

When the crowd outside cleared, we all went inside and chaos erupted. Dad and the captain of the guard yelled at Peyton. Aunt Jasmine yelled at Dad to stop yelling. Peyton yelled back at the captain. The only ones not saying anything were Nightshade, Uncle Hesperus, and me. My eyes met my uncle's and a question I had been asking myself since Peyton mentioned it had been answered.

"Stop!" I screamed.

Everyone went silent and looked at me, but my eyes were still on Uncle Hesperus.

"You told me this story when I was a kid. A story about a mythical well that had been sealed long ago by an ancient one called Sythion. The Seal of Sythion, you called it. It's real."

That last part wasn't a question, but Uncle Hesperus nodded anyway.

"Ebony, the story of Sythion is just that. A story," Dad said.

I finally tore my gaze away from my uncle and faced my dad. His eyes were red and dull. Like the life had completely left him when Mom died. I couldn't look at him without tears threatening to fall, so I looked at the ground as I spoke.

"I tried to save her. I screamed and screamed, but no one was there to help. She loved you, Dad. I know she did. And I'm so sorry. I'm so—"

Tears fell fast and hard. Footsteps approached, and I looked up as Dad smoothed my hair and kissed my forehead.

"I loved her just as much, and we both loved you."

I took a deep breath and looked into my father's eyes. "I had a dream last night. Well, it was more like a vision dream. I saw Mom, and she told me to tell you that the Seal is real. I'm guessing she knew we would need its power, and she wanted to make sure you knew about it."

Dad's eyes welled up with tears. "You saw her?"

I nodded.

Dad wiped his eyes quickly and turned toward Uncle Hesperus. "Luna always knew what was best, and if she thinks the Seal of Sythion is real and can help, I'll help find it."

"I appreciate the gesture, Horus," my uncle said. "And as much as Ebony would like to think that message was for you, I think it was for her."

My eyes widened. "Me? What makes you say that?"

"Visions don't normally have dead people in them. And the dead definitely don't talk. I don't think what you had was a true vision, but someone using your ability to speak to you through someone you trust."

"What does that mean?" It was the first time Nightshade has spoken this entire time, but now he came up behind me and put his hands on my shoulders.

Uncle Hesperus sighed. "It means that we have no choice but to look for the Seal of Sythion. Because I think someone else already is."

CHAPTER SIX

THAT NIGHT, AFTER UNCLE Hesperus sent the captain of the guard home, the rest of us sat around the table in the living room and planned how to find the Seal of Sythion.

"Where do we even start with this?" I groaned.

Uncle Hesperus rubbed his chin. "We need information. The royal library is bound to have something we can use."

"We do not have the time for research," Nightshade argued. "If someone else is already looking for the Seal, then we have to move quickly."

"We split up," Dad said. "Half of us go looking for the Seal while the other half researches as much as they can."

Aunt Jasmine shook her head. "That leaves the human world undefended."

They argued back and forth for a while, but no one came to any conclusion about how to protect the human world, research Sythion, and actually look for the Seal.

I stood up and laid my hands on top of the rough wood of the table. "This is what we're going to do. We split into three groups. Since I'm the one having the visions, I have to go look for the Seal. Nightshade—"

"Will stay here," Peyton interjected. "And I'll go with you on the quest."

"No." Nightshade said through clenched teeth.

"I agree. No." I grabbed Nightshade's hand and squeezed tightly.

"It makes sense," Peyton said, "I don't know the human world like you all do, and I find reading absolutely boring."

Nightshade's hand was trembling with rage in my ownm. I squeezed a bit tighter to let him know I was with him. Always.

He pulled his hand out of my grasp, and I swallowed hard.

Uncle Hesperus stood up and clasped his hands behind his back. He split us up into our groups, and the tone of his voice said there would be no more arguments.

Peyton and I would head out on the mission to find the Seal while Dad and Uncle Hesperus would go back to Amethystia and research all they could on the Seal and Sythion himself. Aunt Jasmine and Nightshade would stay here in the human realm and keep the demons at bay for as long as possible.

After we had ironed out the plan, we all went to bed. Nightshade didn't stay with me that night, and I knew he was still hurt about the night before. Peyton, however, came into my room with a pillow and a blanket under his arm.

"What in the hell are you doing?" I demanded.

"Well, since your boy toy doesn't want to be your bodyguard right now, I guess I'll have to fill in." He plopped the pillow down on the floor and spread the blanket out.

"I don't need a bodyguard," I mumbled as I turned my back to him.

"And yet, I don't see you arguing." Peyton flopped down noisily onto the makeshift bedroll and stretched out.

"Is there any point in arguing with you?"

"Nope."

I almost heard his smile, and I squeezed my eyes shut. Maybe I could will myself to sleep.

"You know, it's going to be dangerous." Peyton's voice was unusually somber, and I rolled back toward him.

"I know, but it's not like I haven't been in dangerous situations before."

Peyton sighed. "You don't get it. The Seal of Sythion... well, let's just say I know more than most people about what it can do and how dangerous it can be."

I lifted an eyebrow. "How?"

Peyton put his arms behind his head and closed his eyes. "Doesn't matter. Get some sleep. You'll need it."

I tried to do as Peyton said, but my mind was buzzing. Who was Peyton, anyway? I had never seen him use magic, so if he wasn't a witch, then what was he? And how did he know so much about the Seal? Those questions and more swirled around in my head as I drifted off to sleep, but sleep didn't last long as a noise downstairs jolted me awake.

Peyton and I rushed into the living room to find Nightshade and Sam locked in battle. Well, battle wasn't exactly the right term. It was clear Sam had trained to fight these last months, but Nightshade had been training a lot longer and his muscle memory took over. Sam, though, was still thinking through the moves he would make, and how to follow through. The fight was clumsy, but it was definitely still a fight. Peyton held me back as I rushed over to help. I struggled against him, but his grip tightened.

"This is Nightshade's job. You would only get in the way," Peyton said.

All I could do was watch in horror as the two men exchanged blows. Uncle Hesperus burst in and flung Sam into the next room with a defense spell. Sam got to his feet, albeit shakily, and breathing hard, as he and Nightshade stared each other down.

"Sam, what are you doing here?" Uncle Hesperus asked calmly.

"I was told to deliver this." He held up a piece of paper for us to see.

"And you couldn't have done it in the morning?" Peyton asked.

Sam didn't even look at him, though I was sure it was to avoid looking at me.

"We'll take the note." Aunt Jasmine strode into the room and held out her hand.

Sam laid the note in her hand and, without another word, marched out of the house.

We all huddled around the living room table while Aunt Jasmine unfolded the note and read it aloud. "Do not look for the Seal of Sythion. Not only will it be the last thing you do, but poor Sam will pay the price."

I rubbed my temples. "Sam delivered a letter... threatening his own life?"

"Maybe someone forced him to deliver it," Nightshade mused.

"Or he could have written it himself to throw us off his tracks," Peyton suggested.

"How could Sam have known we were even going to look for the Seal?" My head spun. I felt like if I didn't sit down soon, my legs would give out.

Peyton pursed his lips but said nothing further.

"So, what do we do?" Aunt Jasmine asked Uncle Hesperus.

"The plan hasn't changed. We will find the Seal of Sythion before someone else does, but we also need to be wary. We're being spied on, and I don't like that prospect."

Everyone went back to bed to get as much sleep as they could, but Nightshade slipped out onto the deck and I followed.

"Thank you for holding back with Sam," I said.

Nightshade didn't answer. Instead, he looked up at the late spring sky and sighed.

I took a deep breath of the crisp night air, and looked up at the stars with him. His hand flexed at his side, and he pulled away as I reached for it.

"I cannot do this," he said.

I looked at him with confusion clearly written on my face. "Can't do what?"

Nightshade looked into my eyes, and I saw sadness and... resignation in them. "I cannot be your bodyguard and your boyfriend. They conflict with each other. No matter how much I wish I could, I cannot be both. So I have decided to be neither."

The air went cold. "What do you mean by 'neither'?"

Nightshade swallowed. "When you leave here tomorrow, I will no longer be your bodyguard. Or your boyfriend."

"You're... you're breaking up with me?" I hugged myself.

This couldn't be happening. Nightshade loved me and I loved him. That was enough.

It had to be.

Nightshade nodded, and I couldn't get air into my lungs. The world spun and there was a roaring in my ears. I didn't want to hear any more. I ran up to my room and flung myself onto my bed and let the sobs take over. My door opened and Peyton was by my side in an instant, asking me what was wrong, but I couldn't talk. I couldn't think. This was wrong. This couldn't be real. Peyton tried to get my attention once more, but when I wouldn't respond for the second time, he slammed the door and left. He was probably going to sleep in the hall or somewhere where my sobs wouldn't keep him awake, but I knew I wasn't getting any sleep that night.

Dawn broke, and my face was puffy. I had been crying all night, so it was no surprise when I went into the bathroom and my face looked like several bees had stung it. I put a cool washcloth over it to bring down the swelling. When I thought I looked presentable enough, I went downstairs and stopped dead when I walked into the kitchen. Nightshade sat at the table, eating a bagel and sporting a big black eye. I wanted to ask him what happened, but when I opened my mouth to speak, I couldn't form words. I said nothing as I grabbed a mug from out of the cabinet and poured myself some coffee.

Walking out of the kitchen and away from Nightshade felt impossible. My heart squeezed. I just wanted to go over to him, wrap my arms around his neck, and drink in his scent. But I forced myself not to think about it and walk out into the living room where Dad and Aunt Jasmine were sitting on the couch looking at a book.

"What are you guys looking at?" I asked as I sipped my coffee.

"Your aunt found an old photo album of her and your mother," Dad said.

I sat down next to them and looked at a photo of my aunt and my mom sitting next to each other with big smiles on their faces.

"You two look so happy," I said.

I looked at another picture where my mom had a giant grin on her face and someone in the background looked furious.

"What's up with this picture?" I asked, pointing at it.

"Your mom set off a weather bomb in the school gym, and we took this right after," Aunt Jasmine explained. "The principal was so upset she suspended your mother for two weeks."

"Mom set off a weather bomb in school?" My eyebrows shot straight up.

"Oh yeah, your mother was pretty reckless back then."

"Like someone else we know," Dad chimed in.

I thought my mom was so uptight and rigid because she hated how I behaved, but maybe she acted that way because she saw herself in me and didn't want me making the same mistakes. The thought made me feel less alone, and I smiled.

Uncle Hesperus came into the living room and told us it was time to go. My smile disappeared as quickly as it came. We were all gathered in the living room to say our goodbyes, but Nightshade wouldn't acknowledge me. I didn't think my heart could break any more than it already had, but another crack splintered through it. Ignoring the pain, I straightened my spine. I wouldn't let him see me wallow.

My pocket felt heavy as I remembered what I had put in there the night before. I fished it out and clasped the glittering triple moon pendent around my neck. The pendent of the Delacroix family. My family. Aunt Jasmine noticed me put it on and smiled slightly. She knew I had a problem with my bloodline—our bloodline—being a part of a family so evil, and she knew I hadn't yet come to terms with being kept in the dark about it all my life. But if this Seal was so powerful that it could end all magic, then I needed all the magic I could get on my side.

Uncle Hesperus opened the portal to Amethystia and walked through. My dad followed and then Peyton. I was about to join them, but I turned around and hugged Aunt Jasmine tightly. I didn't know when, or if, I would see her again and I didn't want to go without a proper goodbye.

"I love you," I said.

She squeezed me tighter. "I love you too. Your mother would be so proud of you."

I took a deep breath and let go. I let myself glance at Nightshade only once before stepping through the portal.

CHAPTER SEVEN

AMETHYSTIA GREETED ME AS I stepped into the entryway of the palace. Dad, Uncle Hesperus, and Peyton were all waiting as the portal closed behind me.

Peyton glanced at the pendent that sat on my sternum, and I could see he had questions. I would definitely be getting the third degree from him when we were alone.

I walked up to the trio and crossed my arms. "Where do we start looking for the Seal?"

"The stories have all centered on the westernmost part of the Elder Woods." Dad said.

Peyton scoffed. "The Elder Woods, too, are a mythical place."

Uncle Hesperus raised an eyebrow. "Yes, but there is also another mythical wooded area that is not so mythical." He shot me a knowing look.

"The Glade of the Hanged Man," I said.

Uncle Hesperus nodded. "It might be time to confer with the spirit there again. Do you still have the map of the area Nightshade's mother gave you?"

I sighed. "No. It got turned to ash when I was fighting Fabian, but I think I know of someone who can help."

"Who?" Dad asked.

"When Sam and Melissa were here, we kind of ran into a group of bandits. The leader, Warwick, knew where the Glade was. That's how we found it the first time."

"Wait," Peyton said. "Warwick, as in green eyes, scars across his face, looks like he could uproot a tree with his bare hands? That Warwick?"

"You know him?" I asked.

"Well, yeah. We did a couple of... jobs together." He glanced at my uncle and then turned his attention back to me. "I know his haunts. I can get us there."

"Great. We leave now. Dad, Uncle Hesperus, let us know if you find something."

I grabbed Peyton's hand and hauled him toward the gate to the palace. He pulled me to a stop and reminded me about the protestors still outside. I groaned and stalked toward the back gate, where no one save for the royal family could go.

We got about three yards outside the perimeter when I heard a voice that made me want to vomit.

"I knew you would come out this way eventually."

I whirled on Evan and thrust out my palm. "*Magicae!*"

A ball of purple magic flew in his direction, but he dodged it right as it was about to hit him in the face. "You've lost your touch, Ebony."

"Come near me again and you'll see that I really haven't." I grabbed Peyton's hand again, his warmth making my heart sputter, and I noticed he was studying Ethan with an intensity I had rarely seen from him. I nearly ran for the city square, and Peyton followed.

"Not even your Regelf of a boyfriend can protect you from what's coming, Princess!" Evan yelled behind us.

I ignored him, but Peyton chuckled beside me. "You have quite the luck with men. It's entertaining to watch."

I stopped and whirled on Peyton. "What do you mean by that?"

"Oh, don't pretend. We both know why you were crying last night, and why you look like you didn't get a wink of sleep."

I dropped Peyton's hand as if it were ice that burned me. "I-I don't know what you're talking about."

Peyton grabbed me by the waist and held me tight to his body. He leaned down to whisper in my ear.

"Did you like the sight of Nightshade with that shiner I gave him?"

My heart stuttered again. I pushed away from him and he chuckled once more. "You're an absolute asshole."

"But it makes life so much more fun that way."

I yelled and hit him in the chest. He just smirked down at me like I was a child throwing a tantrum. And maybe I was, but Peyton Levin infuriated me to no end. We walked the rest of the way to the square in silence, and for a few moments, I had some peace.

Peyton directed us to a shady-looking bar at the end of the main square. We ducked inside and the noise from the patrons immediately drowned out everything else. The smell hit my nostrils and made me want to gag. It smelled like a sweaty locker room. A few of the guys nodded to Peyton as if they knew him, and Peyton nodded back. I looked to him for an explanation, but he guided us to the back, where two men were playing pool. One of the men had deep brown skin and blazing green eyes. Warwick. He had gotten several more scars since I'd seen him last, but they didn't seem to bother him. He was smiling and laughing just like he was several months ago. We walked up to the pool table and Warwick's eyes bugged out of his head when he saw me.

"Isn't that something? You really like flirting with trouble, don't you, Amberwood?"

"I don't know who this 'trouble' is, but I know she has fun flirting with me," Peyton said.

Warwick laughed, clapped Peyton on the back. Then he turned to me and wrapped me in a big hug. When he pulled back, his smile disappeared.

"What happened?" he asked.

"We need to get to the Glade of the Hanged Man again. And we need someone to point us in the right direction."

"And you thought that someone would be me? Hate to break it to you, Ebony, but the Glade may no longer be there. I've heard some rumors that a bunch of nasty demons have taken up residence in that area. Huge, fire breathing demons."

My shoulders slumped. I glanced at Peyton, who had a sparkle in his eyes. I groaned.

"We're going to fight huge, fire breathing demons, aren't we?"

Peyton gave me a playful shove. "I thought you wanted adventure."

"No, what I want is to get to the Seal of Sythion alive."

Warwick stilled. "You're looking for the Seal of Sythion? Why?"

I sighed. "Reasons."

Warwick took me by the elbow and hauled me into a quiet—well quieter—corner of the bar. "Ebony... I heard about what happened to your mother. I'm so sorry, but the Seal won't solve your problems. It will only create more."

I glared at him defiantly. "Maybe, but it will at least solve the biggest problems. No one has connected the dots yet, but I saw Sam here. In Amethystia. How did he get here without a portal?"

Warwick paled as he guessed where my train of thought was going. "He had help."

I nodded. "There are witches here that are helping witch hunters in the human world. And if you think they'll stop at the royal family, you're wrong."

"If what you say is true, we can't let anyone know. We don't want to cause a panic."

I ran my hands through my hair. "That's why I have to do this. Not for Mom, not for me, but for all of you. I am part of the ruling family and part of my job is to keep you all safe. No matter what."

Warwick shook his head. "But to take magic away from us... people will go insane."

I knew a lot of criminals who had their magic taken away as a punishment had gone insane. There were a few of them that had even died. I weighed Warwick's words. Was I willing to risk a few lives to save everyone? My mom's screams filled my head, and I had my answer.

"Peyton said that if we end magic, all the witches here will become human. I don't know if I believe that, but I have to try. Now, I'm doing this with or without your help, but it would mean a great deal to me if you could point us toward those demons."

Warwick sighed. "From here, go southwest, then east. You won't be able to miss them. And Ebony, I hope you know what you're doing."

We walked back and Peyton was showing the man who had been playing pool with Warwick a few tricks. When Peyton spotted us, he sauntered to me and raised a questioning eyebrow. I shook my head. I wasn't going to tell him what Warwick and I spoke about. Not just yet, anyway. I didn't trust Peyton's motives and if I was right about witches helping Sam, then I had to be wary about who I trusted with the information. Peyton and I walked out of the bar.

"What did Warwick say?" Peyton asked.

"He said to head southwest."

Peyton matched my stride. "What's the plan?"

I sighed. "I don't know, but we have plenty of time to figure it out."

CHAPTER EIGHT

THE TREES WERE DENSE as we made our way through the forest. The air was warm and sweat dripped down the back of my neck as we cleared the way of brush and branches. A deep guttural growl broke the silence, and Peyton and I took cover behind a thick tree. He pressed his body up against mine, and I tried not to think of how his scent mixed with the smell of the wood. I didn't want to admit that it was intoxicating. We looked around each side of the tree and saw a clearing. There were indistinct shapes in the middle of the clearing, and they looked like they were on fire. That couldn't be right.

Peyton gave me a hand signal, telling me to go around and corner the demon. I nodded and slowly made my way to the opposite end of the forest. My heart leaped into my stomach at the sight of the demon. Its red skin was literally burning with embers and the smoke that rose from them smelled like sulfur. A forked tongue slithered out between jagged teeth and its four eyes were black voids.

My palms grew sweaty. My pale face, twisted with fear caught Peyton's eye. He gave me a nod of encouragement and I took a deep breath, the sulfur burning my lungs. We were about to ambush the demons when I saw they had captured some prey. It was a girl with blonde hair... Valerie. What was she doing here? Peyton saw her just as I did, and his face tightened. We had to rescue Valerie and then take out the demons. But how?

Peyton mouthed something to me, but I didn't know what he was saying. I gave a thumbs up anyway, and he gave me a cocky smile. Then he ran toward the demons and started making noise.

He was the distraction, I realized. I took my chance and stalked toward Valerie while the demons howled and slashed their claws at Peyton. Valerie saw me and screamed, but I held a finger to my mouth, signaling her to be quiet. She obeyed, and I crept to her. The demons had bound her in a slimy white substance, and pulling on it did no good. Peyton screamed, and I whirled toward him, only to see him get tossed into the trunk of a thick tree trunk and fall down in a heap.

"Hurry!" Valerie shouted.

That drew the attention of one of the demons, and I swore. Its four eyes narrowed on me and it charged as I kept trying to pull the white substance off Valerie. It was no good, and I had to leap out of the way to keep from getting skewered by large fangs. The demon turned towards me again and I threw a fireball at it.

"*Ignis sphaera!*"

The fireball made direct contact with the demon's face, but it didn't even look bothered by the attack.

"It's... made of fire," Peyton croaked from where he was still slumped by the tree.

So, fire wouldn't work on the creature. Great. I tried to think of another way to defeat it, but it charged again and I had to duck and roll. I rolled right into a steaming pile of its waste and had to keep myself from gagging. The demon turned to charge me again, but its nostrils flared. Like it was sniffing for me. It trudged over, and I stood completely still.

The demon got right in my face and sniffed again. It was like it couldn't decide if I was prey or not. It decided not when Peyton threw a rock at it, hitting it square in the flank. The demon rushed Peyton, and I had an idea. If fire wouldn't work on it...

I ran as fast as I could, trying to get to the demon before it could smash Peyton into a pancake.

"Hey, four-eyed fire starter! Over here!"

The creature stopped its attack on Peyton and whirled on me. My heart thudded in my chest and my hands were shaking at my sides. I knew this was going to be a long shot, and I had never used this spell before, but it had to work. As the demon rushed me, I took a deep breath in and thrust my arm out in front of me.

"*Pruina ruinam!*"

Shards of ice protruded from my hand like thousands of spears, hitting the demon in several places. Everywhere the ice touched, it sizzled and burned. The demon howled in pain and I used the spell again and again until the creature fell and didn't get back up.

I rushed over to Peyton, who was already getting on his feet, and together we ran to Valerie.

"Get me out of this!" she yelled.

We pulled and pulled at the white slime, but the more we tried to dig her out, the more we got stuck ourselves.

"This isn't working," I continued to strain at the slime. "We need to try something else."

"What about frying it off?" Peyton suggested.

I shook my head. "The slime might be combustible."

Valerie flinched, digging herself deeper into the slime. "Please don't make me explode."

Peyton sighed. "Any other ideas?"

I looked at the white slime. We couldn't pull it off and we couldn't use fire on it. I could try using my ice spell again, but the shards might hit Valerie accidentally. I pursed my lips and ran my hand through my waste-encrusted hair.

Aunt Jasmine wanted me to learn some spells handed down from the Delacroix family and I had initially refused. I had wanted nothing to do with that part of my family, but if it helped Valerie...

"I have an idea."

I dug my hands into the slime and concentrated. "*Congelatio.*"

Ice splintered outward from my hands, coating the slime in a layer of frost. I freed my hands and picked up a branch that Peyton broke when he the demon flung him into the tree. I pulled my arms back and swung the branch at the slime, shattering it into a million pieces.

Valerie cried as she sank to her knees. Peyton squatted in front of her and offered her his hand. She took it, and he helped her up.

"Thank you," she said.

"What are you even doing here?" I put my hands on my hips.

Valerie swallowed hard. "I followed you guys through that swirling thing, then I followed you all the way to the bar. I heard where you were headed, and I thought if I got here first, I could help. But that demon thing attacked me, and here we are."

"That shouldn't have been possible. There were people watching us as we left. They would have seen you."

Valerie hesitated, not meeting my eyes, and Peyton laughed. I shot him a look to shut up, but he laughed harder. I sighed.

"That was very dangerous. What about your dad? Where does he think you are?"

Valerie's face turned guilty. So, her dad didn't know she was even gone. I leaned my head back and groaned.

"We're taking you home," I snapped.

"No!" Valerie cried. "Please let me come with you and help. I'll stay out of the way. I promise."

I rolled my eyes. "Amethystia is no place for a human... trust me."

Peyton looked at me like he knew exactly what I was talking about.

"She's right," Peyton said. "We're taking you home. Now."

"No." Valerie crossed her arms in defiance. "You can't make me."

Peyton smirked, and I groaned again. Peyton grabbed my arm and led me over to a place where Valerie couldn't hear us.

"Maybe it's best if she comes with us."

I looked at him incredulously. "Are you out of your mind? She's a kid! And human. She wouldn't last two days here."

"She'll just try to come back on her own, and she won't have anyone to protect her here if she does."

I pursed my lips as I thought. I studied Valerie, who had her face set in determination. There was something else there too. Her legs wobbled a bit, like she was going to take off any other sign of danger.

I threw my hands up. "Fine. We'll watch out for her, but if things get too dangerous, I'm sending her home."

"Agreed."

We sauntered back over to Valerie and when she saw our faces, her eyes lit up. She threw her arms around my neck and squeezed.

"Thank you, thank you, thank you," she squealed.

I hesitantly patted her back, and she let go.

"So, where do we start?" She picked some of the slime that didn't freeze out of her hair.

"We're going to a magical glade to get some answers." Peyton said.

Valerie's face filled with excitement. "That's so cool."

I sighed and together, the three of us went east to find the Glade of the Hanged Man.

CHAPTER NINE

S EVERAL HOURS PASSED WITHOUT even a hint as
to where the glade might be, and the sun was
sinking low on the horizon. Valerie was getting
tired, but we couldn't stop and rest. We *had* to find
it. Peyton looked at me with concern, and when he
mentioned we should regroup, I brushed him off.

He took hold of my arm and jerked me to a stop.
"Hey, both Valerie and I are tired, and I can tell
you are, too. We'll find the glade, but it won't be
tonight. Let's stop and rest."

I pulled my arm away and examined Valerie. She
had been through so much today, and she looked
like hell. I reluctantly agreed with Peyton. Besides,
I needed a shower. We found a place to camp by
a stream and I immediately went into the water
and washed as much of the gunk off as I could.
When I returned to the campsite, Peyton had built

a fire and Valerie was staring at the flames. I sat down beside her and hoped the fire would dry me off soon.

"I'm sorry. I should have realized you're not accustomed to this. It's just... it's been a long six months for me. I want to be done with all of this. The fighting, people dying. It's too much."

Valerie nodded, and Peyton watched us closely. I warmed my hands by the flames.

Peyton stood up. "I should go get us some dinner."

I admired his backside as Peyton strode away, until it was just me and Valerie.

"How are we going to sleep?" she asked. "We have no sleeping bags, and no tent."

I looked up. The stars shone through the thick canopy of trees and Valerie followed my gaze.

"Oh."

I smiled at her. "Not as glamorous as you thought it would be, huh?"

She shook her head, and I laughed. Peyton came back with several fish in his hands, and I wondered how he had caught them all. He skewered them on small sticks and put them against the fire to cook.

I took mine from the fire when the skin was almost burnt and chowed down.

"I'll take first watch tonight," Peyton said as he chewed on his fish.

I watched as the light from the fire danced across his curly brown hair, making it shimmer in hues of red. I wanted to run my hands through those curls.

"Thank you for... for taking care of me. And Valerie. I mean... I'm just going to eat my fish."

Peyton chuckled and his eyes softened. "Of course. I'll always take care of you. And Valerie."

I gave him a half smile and ate in an awkward silence until I couldn't take it anymore. I lay down on the bed of leaves and twigs and cursed myself. I shouldn't have been thinking of Peyton that way. Not when I still loved Nightshade. And I did still love him. The thought of not being near him tightened my chest. I rolled over on the leaves and shut my eyes tight. It wasn't the most comfortable thing in the world, but I fell asleep soon after.

I was dreaming about a pair of light purple eyes when a bright light woke me. Sounds of a woman singing wafted through the trees and I looked around, dazed. I got up, shook the leaves out of my hair and found Peyton facing the direction the light was coming from. When I asked him what was going on, he shushed me. I stuck my tongue out at him. The singing got louder, and I turned my attention to where a woman was tending to her long, curly white hair. Her white dress flowed as if there was an invisible wind fluttering the fabric.

"Solara."

She turned her attention to me. "Hello Ebony. It's been a long time."

I walked toward her. "The last time we met you said it wasn't the time for questions. I believe now is the time."

Solara smiled. "I believe so too, but I already know what you came to ask me. You want to know about the Seal of Sythion, but before you learn about the seal, you need to learn about Sythion himself."

"What about him?" Peyton asked.

Solara turned her attention to him. "Sythion is the founder of all magic. He has tricks up his sleeve to make even the most careful of witches do his bidding. The Seal is no different. It will try to trick your senses, make you think things are there that aren't."

"How do we break the Seal?" I asked.

"Even I do not know that. There are some texts that suggest a way, but those tomes have been lost for decades."

"What if we find them?" Peyton asked.

Solara looked at him, and her eyes glazed over. "Peyton Levin. Your future is clouded. So many choices ahead of you. Be wise, or you will not like the outcome."

Peyton frowned and stuffed his hands in his pockets. Solara faced me again and gave me a grim smile.

"Sythion has become godlike to many people and his ego shows it. He will try whatever tactics he has, and he has many, to stop you from destroying the Seal. Be wary of the company you keep, Ebony. You will need an ally and your magic to stop him. *All* of your magic."

She glanced at the triple moon pendent glittering on my sternum.

With that cheery warning, Solara and the glade disappeared, leaving us in the forest's darkness.

Valerie was still sleeping peacefully. How could she have slept through that? Peyton started the fire again as we probably wouldn't be going back to sleep soon.

"What do you think she meant by all that?" I asked.

Peyton stoked the fire. "Who knows? She could have been making all that up."

I grazed the pendent. "I don't think so."

Peyton noticed my hand. "I think she was right about one thing. You need to come to terms with who you are, or we might not finish this mission."

I looked him in the eye. "The Delacroix family is responsible for the mess we're in right now. How am I supposed to come to terms with the fact that *I* am also responsible?"

Peyton gave me a half smile. "Because you were not responsible. Fabian was. And just because you share a bloodline doesn't make you responsible for his actions."

I focused on the flames. He was right, but I couldn't shake the feeling that if it hadn't been for me, both worlds would still be in one piece, and a ton of innocent lives wouldn't have been lost. My teeth clenched, and my body started to tremble.

"I'm disgusted that I share genes with a horrible bloodline."

Peyton sighed. "You know, your family hasn't been the most benevolent of leaders either."

My eyes shot up. "My uncle has been a great leader."

Peyton raised an eyebrow. "Do you think there we be so many protesters outside the castle gates if he was? He's a good uncle, and he loves you, but he is not a righteous king. I mean, he banished you for dueling."

"He banished me for using Soul Sorcery."

Peyton's mouth dropped open. "You actually used Soul Sorcery in a duel?"

I nodded. "Evan thought it would give me an advantage, and it did, but it also got me banished."

I looked away. I didn't want Peyton to see the tears I held back.

Peyton got up, the leaves on the ground rustling beneath his feet as he made his way over to me. I still didn't look at him. He sighed and sat down beside me.

"I'm sorry," he said.

"What do you have to be sorry for? I'm the one who did it."

Peyton grabbed my chin and gently turned my head so I was looking straight at him. His eyes were full of warmth, but there was something behind his expression that I couldn't place.

"You did nothing wrong." Peyton tucked a strand of hair behind my ear. "Evan should have been the one to pay for the duel. Not you."

I smiled, but it didn't reach my eyes. "Thank you."

Peyton glanced between my eyes and my mouth and I thought he was going to kiss me until Valerie snorted in her sleep and he leaned away.

"We should get some rest."

I sighed, and my heart fell a little. I didn't know why, though. It wasn't like I was attracted to Peyton or anything. Nightshade held my heart. I missed him, so why did I want Peyton to kiss me? I lay down and tried not to think about how complicated my love life, or lack thereof, was getting.

Dawn broke, and Valerie, Peyton, and I headed back to the palace. I had gotten some answers, although they left me with more questions, and I needed to talk to my dad.

We returned to the palace around nightfall, after taking several breaks so Valerie could rest, and I found my dad in the study. He was poring over a stack of books and jumped when I tapped him on the shoulder.

"Sorry," I said. "We need to talk to you."

He glanced over my shoulder, where Valerie was hanging back and looking around at the tall bookshelves that littered the walls.

He raised his eyebrow and sighed. "Apparently, there's a lot to talk about."

I smiled sheepishly. "We kind of stumbled upon her in the forest."

Dad scoffed. Peyton stepped forward and put his hand on my shoulder.

"Ebony is telling the truth. Valerie came here on her own, and we saved her from some demons."

Dad ran a hand across his face. "Of course she did. We'll send her home in the morning."

"No!" Valerie's head whipped toward my dad. "I'm not going back. I came here to help, and that's what I plan on doing."

I confronted her. "You were almost demon chow earlier. Don't you want to go home where it's safe?"

"Safe? You think the human world is safe? My mom died thanks to how *safe* it is."

My heart stuttered. No wonder she was so adamant about helping us end magic.

"I'm sorry. I didn't know."

Valerie crossed her arms. "Well now, you do."

Dad sat in one of the oversized leather armchairs and crossed his legs. "It's up to you, Ebony. Do you want her to stay?"

I examined Valerie. The sound of Fabian electrocuting Melissa popped into my head and I had to squeeze my eyes shut to block out the memory. My heart tightened, and my lips trembled. Taking a deep breath to steady myself, I opened my eyes to find Valerie staring at me pleadingly. I would not make that mistake again. I *would* keep Valerie safe. Even if that meant she was here, where I could monitor her.

"She can stay."

Valerie threw her arms around me and squealed. I hesitantly patted her back. I was so going to regret this. Peyton caught my eye, and I knew he was thinking the same thing.

When Valerie broke the hug, I turned to Dad. "We need to find out more about Sythion. I need to know who he was and how he created magic."

Dad rummaged through his piles of books and handed me and Peyton a stack. "Then let's get to work."

CHAPTER TEN

HOURS PASSED AND NO books had the information we were searching for. I threw the book I was reading across the room, and it landed on the floor with a thud.

"Careful," Dad warned, "These books are old."

"Not old enough," Peyton mused.

Valerie was asleep in the chair next to me and her soft snores filled the room as I thought about what Peyton said. An idea popped into my head and I jumped up and down like a little kid.

"You're a genius Peyton. We need to go older. Dad, wasn't there a library in the old section of the city?"

"The section that is now overtaken by demons?" he asked.

"So, we'll get rid of the demons," I said.

"How?"

"We'll need someone to help. Someone who isn't afraid to use whatever means necessary to rid the area of the demons," Peyton said.

"And who would that be?" Dad asked.

Peyton gave me a look, and I looked at Dad. He threw his head back and groaned.

"I told you years ago I didn't want you around that boy."

"Now we have no choice."

Peyton rose from his chair. "It's getting late. We'll get some sleep and reconvene with this in the morning. Maybe by then we'll have come up with a better solution."

His tone said otherwise, but we all agreed, and I gently woke Valerie. She yawned and stretched her arms. I led her to one of the guest wings. Peyton took the room next to hers and I went to my room. I shut the door behind me and slumped against the wood.

"Now this is a sight. The famous Amberwood witch is exhausted. And here I thought you were invincible."

I straightened and balled my hands into fists as Delilah came out of the shadows.

"How did you get here?" I demanded.

Her tinkling laugh rang through the air. "I have my ways. Just like Valerie has hers."

My eyes narrowed. How did she know about Valerie? Was she a spy for Delilah? No. Valerie was a scared human girl who would never align herself with someone like Delilah.

Delilah sauntered toward me, her pigtails swaying. "Stay out of my way and away from Sam. He doesn't want you anymore, and if you interfere with my plans again... let's just say you won't walk away next time."

I crossed my arm. "Are you threatening me?"

She came so close to me I could smell the bubblegum on her breath. "Duh."

I clenched my teeth as red clouded my vision. This human came into my home, kidnapped and killed my mother, and now she had the audacity to threaten me. I pushed her away and readied a fireball.

"You want to mess with me, bitch? Come get me!" I hurled the fireball past her head and out the window, shattering the glass.

It singed her face, and Delilah howled in pain. She clutched her cheek as rage filled her eyes.

"You'll pay for that, Ebony! You. Will. Pay."

"Put it on my tab." I stalked past her. "Now, if you're done playing games, I would like to go to bed."

A portal opened, and she walked through while my eyes almost popped out of my head. How did she open a portal by herself? She wasn't a witch. Someone must have been helping her. Was it Valerie? I wanted to march right to Valerie's room and demand she tell me how she got to Amethystia, but my exhaustion got the better of me and I hurled myself into bed and fell into a restless sleep.

The next morning Valerie, Peyton and I sat in the dining hall eating breakfast. Valerie gaped in awe at all the food set in front of us. I kept my eyes on her, and Peyton tried to get my attention to see what was going on. I waved him off. He tried to get my attention again, and again, I swatted his hand away. He gave up after that, and I focused my full attention on Valerie. She looked so innocent, so *human,* but was she really, or was she just pretending to be something she wasn't? She noticed me staring, and her brows scrunched in confusion. I gave her a half smile, trying to ease her worries, and she beamed back at me.

After breakfast, the three of us were in the throne room, getting ready to leave for Willowdale, the ancient part of the main city, when Evan walked through the door. I groaned as he swaggered toward us with a cocky grin on his face.

"I heard you need my services. How can I help?"

"You can go die in a hole," I spat.

"Tsk tsk tsk." Evan wagged his finger in my face. "A princess should never speak like that."

I rushed him, but Peyton grabbed me by the waist and pulled me back before my fist connected with Evan's mouth.

Dad and Uncle Hesperus sighed and waited until things calmed down before giving us each a pack of supplies and weapons. Valerie didn't get any weapons, however. Instead, she her pack contained extra water and jerky. She looked disappointed at that, but I was relieved that I wouldn't have to worry about her killing us in our sleep. We left the castle and crept past the crowd of people that were still throwing rotten food at the guards.

The path to Willowdale was long and arduous, the roads worn with years of disrepair. Peyton, Evan, and I hopped easily over the cracked and jagged stones, while Valerie had a more difficult time. Evan dropped back to help Valerie, and I noticed he was extra friendly with her. I rolled my eyes and kept going. Evan would have flirted with anything if given the chance. That was one of the reasons I dumped him. The four of us stopped dead when we heard a loud screeching overhead. The screeching came closer, as did the flapping of immense wings. Several pairs of wings, in fact. I looked up and large pterodactyl-like demons circled us.

"Scatter!" Peyton yelled.

I ran for the nearest boulder, but that was too small to be used as cover. Besides the demons had an overhead view. Valerie screamed as one of them dove down and grabbed at her hair. Evan tried to get the demon's claws untangled from Valerie, but it was no use. The demon flung Valerie in the air and she smashed into a rock as she fell to the ground. She groaned but didn't move. I tried to reach her, but I was dealing with a demon bird of my own. It dove toward me, and I ducked as its claws raked the air where my head had just been.

"We need cover!" Evan yelled.

I looked around frantically until I saw a derelict cottage.

"There!" I pointed, and Evan followed my gaze. He gave me a nod and went straight for the cottage without even looking back. Asshole. Peyton rushed for Valerie and, as gently as he could, picked her up. We ran for the cottage, weaving and dodging between the claws of the demons. We raced inside and slammed the door behind us. The cottage shook with the force of the demon birds repeatedly hitting the siding. Peyton gently laid Valerie down on the musty bed that sat in the room's corner. Her breathing was even, but she had a huge gash in her forehead. Peyton looked for first aid while I stalked up to Evan and slapped him across the face.

"What the hell was that?" I demanded. "You were just going to leave us to die?"

"I was scouting the area."

"That's crap," Peyton said as he rifled through cabinets.

He found the first aid supplies underneath the sink in the kitchen. He ran a cloth under the running water and cleaned Valerie's cut as gingerly as he dared. Valerie stirred, and I let out a silent breath of relief. Even if she was a traitorous piece of filth, she didn't deserve to die. I had been through that before.

The shaking died down and silence fell. We all looked at each other. The silence stretched for seconds, minutes. My muscles relaxed, and I sat down on the side of the bed next to Valerie. I was dabbing her forehead, cleaning the blood off her face when the window blew out, shattering glass everywhere. I covered Valerie's body with mine as a huge beak snapped at us through the now open hole in the cottage. Peyton found a broom and beat the demon with the handle, which seemed to annoy it more than anything else. Evan shot electricity at the demon, helping Peyton beat it back enough for me to put a shield around the window.

"We need to leave. We aren't safe here." Peyton gasped.

"We can't leave Valerie." Evan said.

I gaped at him. "Since when are you concerned about anyone but yourself?"

Evan narrowed his eyes at me. "I was concerned about you once. Before you turned into a goody witch."

I balled my hands into fists, ready to knock his teeth out, when Peyton stepped between us.

"Alright, we get it. You two hate each other. Now, can we please figure a way out of this?"

I glanced at Valerie and then turned to Evan. "Help me with her."

Together, Evan and I hauled Valerie out of the cottage and we jogged away from the demons, looking for another safe place to stay.

CHAPTER ELEVEN

WE RUSHED THROUGH WILLOWDALE, the demons hot on our heels. Valerie weighed Evan and me down enough that my legs burned as we ran down the eroded cobblestone street. We saw several buildings, but none of them were safe enough for us to use as shelter. My knees buckled, and I dropped Valerie's legs on the ground with a dull thud. Evan faltered in his steps, and the demon birds screeched in victory. They swooped toward us, claws extended, ready to go in for the kill. I closed my eyes, not wanting to see my own entrails spilled onto the ground when a buzzing in the air caught my attention.

My eyes opened and an elderly woman stood over us, her long, gray hair whipping in the wind. She held a worn wooden staff in the air. Bright silver light emitted from the staff in a gigantic dome around us. The demon birds screeched and scratched at the dome with no luck. It held strong.

The woman reeled the staff back and thrust it toward the demons and shouted, "*Argentum undam!*"

A blast of light shot from the staff in all directions and everywhere the light touched the demons, they burst into ash.

"Get up, child!" the woman shouted. "My home is just over that hill. Go!"

I scrambled to my feet and helped Evan carry Valerie over the hill to the only structure in the entire town that looked like it had been kept up.

Peyton was already inside when we slammed the door open and rushed in. The woman came in seconds later, and with a wave of her hand, the door shut behind her.

"Who—who are you?" I gasped.

"The question, my dear, is who are you?"

I rested my hands on my knees as I huffed from the exertion of carrying Valerie while running for my life. "My name is—"

The woman waved her hand in dismissal. "I know your name, Ebony Amberwood, but who are you?"

"Cut the cryptic crap, old lady." Evan pointed a dagger at the woman's throat. "Who are you?"

Peyton's dagger, I realized. How did he get that thing away from him? Peyton must have realized it was his dagger too, because he casually reached behind him where he normally kept it sheathed and then narrowed his eyes at Evan when it wasn't there.

"My name is Mave. And I am the last resident of this once beautiful part of the city."

I laid my hand on Evan's wrist and had him lower the dagger. He reluctantly did, and I gave the weapon back to Peyton, who promptly put it away.

"What happened here?" I asked.

Mave crossed the room. "Your ancestors."

A vague memory of reading a book in the library back home popped into my head.

My fingers grazed the pendent around my neck. "Alaric Delacroix and Dante Amberwood. This is the spot where they dueled, isn't it?"

Mave nodded. How old was she if she was there to witness that? I didn't have to ask though because she walked to the window and gazed out into the distance.

"Ninety years have passed since their duel and yet no one in the Amberwood family has deigned to repair this part of the city." Her eyes sparkled with life as she whirled toward me. "Yet you are an Amberwood by name and a Delacroix by blood. Perhaps you can end your family's reign of terror after all these years."

"What are you talking about? The Delacroix's reign of terror ended when I killed Fabian."

Evan scoffed, and I narrowed my eyes at him. "Do you have something to say?"

"The reign of terror didn't end with Fabian. It started with your family. Your uncle is the worst by far."

"Say that again and I'll show you what the two most powerful bloodlines mixed can really do."

Evan stalked up to me and got right in my face. "Your uncle has put people, his people, in poverty while he lines his pockets. I'm sorry, lines your pockets."

I stepped back and shook my head. That wasn't true. It couldn't have been true. My uncle loved his people. He would never have taken advantage of them.

Peyton grabbed Evan by the collar and pulled him from me. Evan pushed Peyton away and smoothed his shirt.

Mave cleared her throat, and Evan and Peyton had the decency to look ashamed.

"Fighting amongst friends started the feud between the Delacroixes and Amberwoods in the first place. Let's not repeat history, shall we?"

I shook my head, hoping that it would help clear my thoughts, and squared my shoulders as I turned toward Mave.

"We're on a quest to discover more about Sythion. We were hoping coming here would lead us to the answers we need."

"I know why you've come, but before we talk about that, I must see if you're worthy of the information."

"How do we do that?" Peyton asked.

"A test." Mave's eyes gleamed.

Evan scoffed. "We don't have time for that, old hag. Just tell us what we need to know so we can get out of here."

I rolled my eyes. We were going to get nowhere if Evan kept opening his mouth. I stalked up to Mave.

"What do we have to do?"

"Stay alive."

Peyton came up behind me and whispered in my ear. "This smells like a trap. I don't like it. We'll figure out another way to learn what we need."

I shivered. Whether it was from the warmth of his breath on my neck or his warning, I didn't know. I turned to him and his face was closer to mine than I expected. I glanced at his mouth, which parted slightly. His hands grazed mine, and his pupils dilated. Evan gagged in the distance, breaking the hold that Peyton's closeness had over me.

I leaned toward Mave and took a deep, cleansing breath. "We accept the challenge."

Mave's face changed from a nice and sweet old lady to that of a cold and cunning old crone.

This was going to hurt.

Mave took us around the back of her cottage and, with a wave of her hand, we were in an underground cave with a lake of lava on our right and a sheer cliff face on our left. I could hear screeching in the distance, and I recognized the sound of the demons we encountered earlier.

"Where are we?" Evan asked.

"What do you mean?" Mave asked. "We're outside my cottage. Or have you forgotten?"

Peyton leaped to the ground as one of the flying demons from earlier swooped down and almost took his head off.

"We are not by your cottage!" Peyton shouted. "And why are those things trying to kill us again?"

I whirled toward Mave, and her smile grew. My blood ran cold as I realized why she never had to say a spell to cast magic. Or why it was pure coincidence that those demons had never touched her, even while she was the only one in the area.

"You... you're a demon, aren't you?"

Mave's eyebrows shot up in surprise. "A demon? Hecate no, but I know a trick or two."

Her eyes flickered purple, and as my brain told me we were in danger, my instincts calmed my heart rate. I had been in this type of situation before, and I knew how to handle it. I ran to Peyton and got him off the ground as quickly as I could. Evan was nowhere to be found, so I gripped Peyton's hand tighter and sprinted toward an enormous boulder in front of us. It didn't give us much cover, but at least it would give us enough to talk through a quick plan of attack.

"We need to get out of here," I said.

"Really? What makes you say that? The demons trying to kill us, or could it be the unhinged lady trying to get us killed by demons?"

I rolled my eyes. The screeching got closer, and we had little time before they ate us like a veggie platter.

"Look," Peyton said, "this is all probably an illusion. If we can break the spell, we can get out of here. We'll figure out another way to learn about Sythion, but this is too dangerous."

I had to agree with him, but...

"This is the only way. We have to defeat these demons, so here's the plan—"

The screeching intensified, and I looked up just in time to yell for Peyton to run before demon talons sliced through the air.

We ducked out of our flimsy cover, each going the opposite direction. Peyton screamed and got the demon's attention. My eyes darted across the landscape, searching for Evan, but again, I couldn't find him. I did, however, spot Mave by what looked like the opening to the cave. I had to get around her without being spotted. Peyton was doing a good job distracting the demons, but Mave wasn't paying any attention to him or me. Her gaze was locked on the ceiling. I followed her eyes and froze. Hanging upside down from the rocky roof of the cave were dozens of demons, just like the one Peyton was facing. My heart sank as I realized we might truly be in over our heads with this battle. There was no way we could take on that many demons by ourselves, and without knowing where the rest of our group was, we couldn't take the risk. Another demon had joined the fray, and

Peyton's strength was waning. I needed a strategy. Any strategy.

I whirled around and found Mave directly in front of me. She grabbed my wrist and twisted my arm until I fell to my knees. I screamed in pain as my bones groaned and protested at the movement. Peyton turned toward me, hearing my scream, and one of the demon's claws sunk into his shoulder. Blood spurted from the wound and the sound of his knees hitting the rocky surface made me wince. The cave disappeared, and we were now back in the peaceful garden at the back of the cottage. Mave ordered the demon to fly Peyton off somewhere as she hauled me to my feet and dragged me back inside.

CHAPTER TWELVE

MAVE SHOVED ME AGAINST the wall, and the stone of the cottage grazed my cheek.

"So you are the greatest your bloodlines have to offer?" Her voice was like poison, seeping into my body, holding me to the wall. "I'm not impressed."

"I never wanted to be a part of the Delacroix family," I gasped.

Mave swept her hand across my forehead, wiping away a lock of hair that hung in m eyes. "But you are, dear. And it's a shame that you don't listen to that part of you more. You might have beaten me if you had."

She waved her hand in the air, and my head slammed into the stone. I winced. I couldn't move. It was like someone, some invisible person, was holding me there. I wasn't going to let this shriveled up old hag, as Evan called her, kill me. I would never hear the end of it if I did. Blood trickled down my face, and anger shot through me. White-hot, and volatile. I had felt this once before. On top of the ruins where I fought Fabian. I had to reign that anger in, but... I didn't want to. I wanted to let this mummy of a witch have it.

So I did.

I pushed back against the weight that held me to the cottage wall and I broke through whatever spell holding me there. I whirled around and found a smirk on Mave's face. A smirk I would wipe off if it was the last thing I did.

Warmth spread throughout my body, and that warmth turned to roaring flames. I curled my hands into fists and the windows exploded, glass spraying everywhere. Mave dove to the ground, but I didn't even flinch as shards of glittering glass grazed my skin and left thin red lines down my arms and across my face.

Once the fragments stopped clinking to the floor, Mave got to her feet, her eyes wide with pride.

"I knew you had our blood in you. I could sense it when you first came here."

My eyebrows scrunched inward. Peyton burst into the room, his shoulder leaking blood. I rushed to him and put pressure on the wound, but with a wave of her hand, Mave healed the gashes covering Peyton's skin. We both gaped at her, waiting for an explanation.

She sighed and sat down in a chair in the room's corner. "My name is Mave Delacroix. I am your great-great-grandmother. I saw you having trouble with the demons. I knew you had not yet learned to master your abilities, and I had to see how far you were in your training. As it turns out, your mother hasn't taught you anything, that ungrateful wretch."

The old hag's words were like a knife to my heart. "Don't talk about my mother like that! She was a better witch than you will ever know."

"Was?" Mave's back straightened. "What do you mean 'was'?"

"You don't know?" Peyton asked, his voice dripping with acid.

"I'm not omniscient," Mave spat back.

I took a shaky breath, and reminded myself that while my mom had perished, she had been Mave's family too.

I steadied myself as I stepped between them. "Back to your corners. Please." I turned to Mave. "My mom... died. Very recently."

Mave frowned. "How?"

"Witch hunters," Peyton said.

"It's my fault," I said. "My friend... or he *was* my friend, warned me that if I used magic, he would kill me and my family. I didn't listen."

A tear escaped down my cheek, and I quickly wiped it away. Peyton put his hand on my shoulder and squeezed. Mave's hands balled into fists and the ground beneath us started shaking. Peyton squeezed my shoulders harder as I grabbed onto the nearest object. Which just so happened to be a stuffed elephant next to the bed. My knees buckled from the vibrations, but Peyton's strength held me up.

"Mave, whatever you're doing, stop. I don't know how much more this house can take." Peyton let go of my shoulders and stepped toward Mave. My knees held me, but my teeth rattled so badly I thought I would break a couple of them. Peyton reached Mave and when his hands touched her leathery skin, they glowed. It was the first time I had seen him use magic, and it honestly shocked me. I didn't think Peyton had ever told me what he was, and I never asked. The ground stopped shaking and when I let go of the stuffed elephant, I found I had squished the stuffing so bad there was now a permanent dent in its head. I walked up to Peyton and Mave on wobbly legs, and Mave was now in tears. I halted and knit my eyebrows together. Mave looked like a badass who should never be messed with, and here she was, bawling her eyes out.

"What did you do to her?" I asked.

"I let her feel peace."

"What do you mean?"

"Come here, let me show you."

I hesitantly laid my hand in his outstretched palm.

His fingers wrapped around mine and whispered the words, "*Pax deambulatio.*"

Blue light emitted between his fingers, and my skin warmed. It wasn't uncomfortable in the slightest, though. It was... like being home. My body went slack, and Peyton's arm wrapped around my waist and as he held me to him, there was nothing but the two of us and the sensation of floating.

When the light finally died, I wanted to cry too. I had never felt such peace, and I wondered if that was what it felt like when you died. I hoped it was as it meant my mom felt that way right now.

Mave sniffled, and I turned back to her. Her eyes didn't have as much malice in them, and somehow, she looked a lot younger. Like the weight of the world wasn't on her shoulders anymore. She stood and strolled toward us. She wrapped me in a big hug and my shoulders stiffened at the contact. Mave let me go and turned toward Peyton. "That is one hell of a gift you have. Use it wisely."

I looked around the room and groaned. "Where are Valerie and Evan?"

Mave looked at me sheepishly. "Your friend woke up, and the boy you call Evan took her away. I don't know where they went."

Peyton's jaw tightened, and my hands balled into fists at my side. I'd kill him. I'd dismember him first, but then I'd kill him. Valerie was my responsibility, and knowing who she was with right now made my stomach tighten. Peyton caught my eye and nodded. He was thinking the same thing.

He took a deep breath and smiled at Mave. "We came here for a reason and, well, family ties and stolen girls aside, we need to complete our mission."

Peyton glanced at me, and I cleared my throat. Mave's attention moved to me.

"We're trying to find out about Sythion and the Seal he created, but to do that, we need access to the library here. We were on our way there when we got attacked by those demons."

Mave's face fell. "I'm sorry, but bandits destroyed the library years ago. They pillaged it and burned it down."

My head flung back, and I groaned. Why couldn't anything go our way?

"However," Mave said, tapping her chin. "I grabbed some of the most important tomes and hid them away. There might be something there that can help you."

My eyes lit up, and I felt like I could kiss Mave. Although, that would have been awkward, so I didn't. She motioned for us to follow her, and we went to the back of the cottage to a little room. The room held a table and two chairs that sat on a rug. She asked Peyton and me to move the furniture aside. After we cleared the room, Mave pulled back the rug, revealing a trapdoor in the floor.

"Open it," she said.

Peyton and I looked at each other.

"It's locked," I said.

"I know," Mave said. "Unlock it."

I raised an eyebrow and shrugged as I pulled on the handle. When nothing happened, I gave Mave a look that said "I told you so" and she told me to try again. I pulled and pulled on the handle, but the door didn't budge.

"I locked the door with blood magic. Use your bloodline, *our* bloodline, and open the door."

I took a deep breath in and tried the door once more. It didn't budge. Peyton grabbed my shoulder and squeezed.

"You can do this," he whispered.

Knowing he had faith in me made my body relax. I closed my eyes and felt a familiar tug in my stomach. I had felt that tug when I was looking for the Delacroix family sword. My family sword. I was a Delacroix, even if I didn't like it. I used that pull and tugged on the handle again. It groaned as it opened, and I felt Peyton's breath on my ear as he smiled. Mave looked smug as she flicked her wrist and a ball of light bobbed above her head. She descended the steep stone staircase, and Peyton and I followed.

CHAPTER THIRTEEN

THE BASEMENT WAS SMALL and stuffy as we made our way past troves of old and broken furniture. Mave led us to the back, where a small bookshelf stood. The books were bound in red and green leather with no titles on the spines, but I felt their power. Peyton and I took a book each. He perched himself on a circular table and I sat down in the chair next to him. We cracked open our respective books and started reading. Mave left at some point, but the bobbing light stayed overhead, illuminating the pages so we could read.

Peyton slammed the book shut after about an hour of skimming through its pages and picked another one off the shelf. I shut my book shortly after and went to do the same when I noticed a book sitting on the floor. It looked older than the rest of them, and it was bound in worn, cracked brown leather. I picked it up, and a thrill went through me. I sat back down in the chair, opened the cover, and found Sythion's name written on the first page in dark, swirling calligraphy.

"I think I found something," I said.

Peyton shut his book and leaned over my shoulder to read. I went through page after page of handwritten notes and doodles of demons. I stopped flipping through pages when I spotted a drawing of the Seal. Peyton hopped off the table and grabbed a chair. He situated it right next to me and we were so close, our arms were touching. My breathing picked up a little, and I hoped Peyton didn't notice. I read through the notes in the margins and Peyton and I looked at each other.

"This is how he made the Seal," I said.

"This might tell us how to destroy it," Peyton added.

The book heated in my hands until it felt like my skin was going to burn, and spots danced across my vision. I dropped the book and put my palms to my temples, hoping it would help the pounding pain in my head. No such luck. Pain rippled through me as my vision overtook reality.

I was in the mossy cave again with an old man whom I had never seen before. He had a wispy white beard down to his waist and a red cloak tied around his neck. Perched on the well in the middle of the cave, he gazed at me.

"You're him, aren't you?" I asked, "You're Sythion."

"And you are Ebony Amberwood. You have been causing trouble for me, and I don't like that."

I scoffed. "Trouble? What trouble have I been causing?"

"The Seal that you so desperately seek to destroy is my greatest creation. I have spent thousands of years protecting it."

I raised an eyebrow and crossed my arms. "Then maybe it's time you retire."

Sythion gracefully stepped down from the well's edge, and a flash of sadness crossed his features before he looked at me with disdain.

"I tried to warn you away. I thought seeing your loved ones would be enough to deter you from going down this path, but time and again you have refused, and now I must intervene myself."

"What do you mean?"

"I just mean I have to stop you from destroying everything I worked so hard to create."

Sythion was faster than I would have thought for an old man. He grabbed my arm roughly and muttered some words in a language I didn't understand. It sounded ancient and cold. Stabbing pain shot up my arm and I screamed as thorns protruded from my skin. They wrapped around my arm like a vise grip and I tried to rip my hand away from Sythion's grasp. He held on tighter, and the thorns gripped into my arm like claws. Blood dripped from the wounds, I screamed again, but there was no one around to hear. I could barely think. This was a vision, I reminded myself, and I had to get out of it. I had to get back to reality. Blood was now pouring from my arm and dripping onto the floor in tiny puddles. Using every bit of strength I had, I yanked my arm out of Sythion's grasp. He had a look of utter shock on his face, and I took advantage of the distraction. I took a deep breath and screamed my way out of the vision.

Peyton was cradling me in his arms, on the floor, and Mave stood over us as I opened my eyes. I was back in the basement in Mave's cottage and Sythion's book lay open on the ground.

"What happened?" Peyton's voice was full of concern, and I almost thought he sounded scared.

"I... Sythion pulled me into a vision." I said.

"Through the journal?"

I nodded.

"Interesting," Mave said. "What did he tell you?"

"He told me to back off, and then..." I looked at my arm and I groaned.

Not again. On my arm was a tattoo of black thorns winding its way around my skin. They converged on my palm and ended in a rose so black I thought Sythion had painted it on.

"What is that?" Peyton asked.

"A present from Sythion," I said, "to make sure I don't destroy the seal."

"What does it do?" Mave asked.

I shrugged and got up off the ground. Mave and Peyton helped me stand up and although I felt steady on my feet, my arm felt like it was trembling.

I balled my hand into a fist and then I thrust my hand out, palm facing the ceiling.

"*Ignis sphaera!*"

A fireball appeared in my hand, and I quickly extinguished it.

"Well, he didn't take away my magic," I said, my heartbeat slowing. I didn't think I'd be able to handle not having magic again.

"So, what *did* he take?" Mave mused.

Peyton and I looked at her. I balled my hands into fists, covering the rose now inked on my palm. If Sythion took something from me, I would find out what and I would take it back.

I snatched the journal off the floor. "We should get back to Dad and Uncle Hesperus. We need to fill them in on everything that's been going on."

Peyton nodded, but Mave grabbed my arm. "Let the boy take the journal back to the palace. I would like to teach you some tricks that may help you along your journey."

I glanced at Peyton, and he shrugged, leaving the choice up to me. I nodded and handed the book to Peyton.

"Be careful," he warned, his hand lingering on my skin.

"I will be."

With that, he turned and went back up the steps to the main house.

Mave sat me down on the dusty couch and grabbed a hold of my hand. She turned the tattoo over and gazed at it for a long time.

"Do you know what it does?" I asked.

Mave shook her head. "No, but if Sythion branded you, it must have been for a reason."

I sighed. Of course it was for a reason, but for what reason? What could he possibly want to keep me from doing?

Mave stood up, and I followed her back inside the main house. She locked the door behind her, and we moved the furniture back. To the ordinary eye, it would look like an ordinary room, with a table and two wooden chairs. We went out the back and with a wave of her hand, Mave turned her garden into a training facility. Straw dummies appeared. Mave staggered them at even intervals and set up colored targets high and low. Some had the bullseye scorched, while others were barely hanging on by a thread. Mave stood by my side and taught me a few basic spells I already knew, but then she added in a twist.

"Do the spells without saying anything."

I raised an eyebrow. "I can't."

She hurled a bolt of pure purple magic at one of the dummies, decapitating him. She raised an eyebrow back at me as if to say "See? It's possible."

I groaned and turned to the dummy. I concentrated all my willpower and flung my hand out toward the dummy's straw head. Again, nothing happened. Mave stood behind me and put her hands on my shoulders.

"Concentrate. *Feel* it in your bones and will it into being."

Mave gave me one last squeeze before she let go and moved far away from me. I squared my shoulders and closed my eyes. Fresh air filled my lungs and the sweet smell of the flowers just beyond the illusion entered my nostrils. I imagined Nightshade and me back in the underground garden of the palace, stealing a moment for ourselves, his lips on mine. I imagined a glowing ball of pure magic filling my hands, then opened my eyes and flung my hands out. Bright purple beams of magic spewed from my palms and not only took the dummy's head off, but completely disintegrated the other two dummies on either side of it.

Mave's eyes filled with pride and awe as she strolled back to me. "That was... more than I was expecting."

"Me too" I huffed.

I put my hands on my knees and sank to the ground. Mave helped me to my feet.

"Do it again," she said.

I let my head roll back but did as she requested.

CHAPTER FOURTEEN

THE SUN WAS WELL below the horizon and I was dripping with sweat when Mave finally called me in for dinner. I hobbled through the stone doorway and practically collapsed on the floor in front of the woodstove.

"Get up, girl, or you're going to get burned," Mave scolded.

"What do you mean, *going* to get burned? I'm already burning in hell."

Mave let out a chuckle and nudged my leg over so she could open the oven door. She took out a roasted fire pheasant and placed it on the table. I jumped up and rushed to a chair, and Mave slapped the back of my hand as I reached for the serving spoon.

"Use your magic. Without using your words, serve yourself."

I flung my head back and groaned. No more training. I gave Mave the stink eye, but did as she instructed. With my palm facing up, I willed my plate to be full of food. My magic tried to obey, but my energy was waning, and I flopped my hand onto the wood surface.

"I'm so tired. Can't I just eat and go to bed?"

Mave put her hands on her hips. "Of course you can. But you have to use your magic to do those things."

"Why?"

Mave raised her eyebrow at my whiny tone. I took a deep breath and asked again. Mave jabbed at the tattoo on my arm.

"Do you think Sythion put that thing on your arm for no reason? Do you think when you face him, and you *will* face him at some point, that he's going to let you off easy because you're *tired*?"

I slammed my hands on the table. "If I'm in that type of situation, I *will* be the one to walk away. Make no mistake about that."

"Then show me."

I clenched my teeth and balled my hands into fists. The fire pheasant exploded all over the table, Mave, and me. Both of us recoiled and I yelped.

"Control your emotions," Mave commanded.

"I'm trying. I'm tired, and my magic is almost spent."

Mave gave me a crooked smile. "Not from where I'm standing."

I jumped up and marched over to Mave. "You said you would help me train and become stronger. Now quit being a cryptic bitch and actually help me."

"You've already become stronger, faster than I thought possible. But you aren't strong enough to take on the challenges that await you. Now, since you've ruined our dinner, your room is at the end of the hall. Go."

My mouth dropped open. "You're sending me to bed without dinner? Who are you, my mom?"

Mave got right up in my face. "I'm the only one standing between you and your ability to break that seal. Don't think I'm doing this just for your sake, Ebony Amberwood. There are forces beyond your wildest imagination at work right now, and you are our best chance at stopping them."

I took a step back. "What do you mean?"

Mave sighed and pinched the bridge of her nose. "Never mind. Go to bed. We'll resume training in the morning."

I marched off down the hallway and found my room right where she said it would be. I slammed the door and gasped. The room was completely empty, save for a mattress, a wooden chest in the corner, and a small dresser. I sighed and plopped down on the mattress, sending up a cloud of dust. I jumped up, coughing and silently cursing Mave for making me use more magic when I was so exhausted.

I looked around the room for a comforter and some sheets but found none. I examined the chest. A large iron padlock sealed the chest shut. No matter how hard I pulled, the lock wouldn't open. I even tried blood magic, but no luck there either. I screamed and stomped my foot, sending up even more dust. If Mave wanted to play that game, fine. I would play that game.

"*Concutere!*"

Nothing.

I closed my eyes and took a few deep breaths. In and out. In and out. When my heart rate calmed some, I opened my eyes and concentrated on the lock of the chest. I reached out to it in my mind and willed it to unlock. The lock clicked open, and I sighed. The chest then exploded into a thousand pieces, making me shriek and duck for cover. I stood up and huffed. There was a neatly folded colorful quilt beside a fluffed pillow and a set of pale yellow sheets. How they withstood the explosion I didn't know and didn't dare ask. I quickly made the bed and gave Mave the finger as I fell asleep.

Blaring light woke me the next morning, but it wasn't from the sun. Mave pushed me out of bed and out into the garden before I even had a chance to eat breakfast.

"What time is it?" I yawned.

"Four-oh-three. Now get to work. I'll be back out in two hours." Mave shut the door to the cottage behind her, and it disappeared. I turned back around, and newly built straw dummies stared at me. I groaned, but started trying to hack off their flammable body parts without using spells.

Time passed and Mave came back out to a pile of burnt hay and dismembered dummies.

"Good," she said. "Now we eat."

Like the night before, she wanted me to serve breakfast with my magic, and I did a pretty decent job of not exploding our food. The riverbird eggs were delicious after not eating all yesterday, and I savored every bite until Mave waved her hand and the entire table, including the bite of food I was about to put in my mouth, dissolved into light. This woman was going to get slapped one of these days.

We were again out in the garden, but this time she didn't turn it into a training ground. The garden transformed into a beautiful oasis full of lush green plants and wildlife roaming freely. I took off my shoes and basked in the oasis's warmth. The sand felt amazing between my toes and the salty sea air filled my lungs as I took a deep breath.

"Why did you bring us here?" I asked.

Mave gave me a wicked look. "To show you what you'll be missing. You will be over there."

She pointed to an area on the left that was devoid of any life, save for one lonely coconut tree. "Turn that into this and your training for the day will be done."

I stared at her like she had lost her mind, because it seemed like she actually had.

"I can't turn nothing into"—I gestured wildly around me—"this."

Mave, once again ready to prove me wrong, flicked her wrist and a tiny tree sprouted from the sand.

"Everything comes from something. Do it."

"No."

Mave raised an eyebrow. "Do it."

I raised my chin in defiance. "No."

Mave crossed her arms. "Do you want to learn how to go up against Sythion or not?"

"I do, but the whole point of destroying the Seal is to destroy magic, and it seems all you're teaching me is how to harness it better."

Mave gave me a smirk, and my face fell. "You… don't want me to destroy magic, do you?"

"I actually do." Mave threw her arms in the air. "How old do you think I am, Ebony?"

I looked her up and down. She was obviously older than my mom, but not ancient. If what she told us about her, witnessing the duel between my ancestors was correct… "You're older than you look, I know that."

"I am one thousand five hundred and fifty-two. I have seen the rise and fall of many royal families. Some of them were benevolent, but most of them were not. I have seen my family die several times over, and I'm tired."

My eyes drifted to the tiny tree that stood between us. "How is it you have been alive for so long?"

"I was once in love, and that love cursed me. Literally." Mave's voice sounded far away, but my eyes stayed on the swaying leaves of the magically concocted tree.

"He was Sythion's great-grandson, and he was the most handsome man I had ever seen. We fell in love and were to be married. Sythion found out and forbade the union, but we snuck away and eloped. Sythion's wrath was swift. He killed his great grandson right in front of me and cursed me with immortal life, so I may never forget the cost of crossing him. He didn't give me eternal youth and beauty though, and so I have been slowly withering away decade after decade."

Tears streamed down Mave's face.

I swallowed hard. Mave must have been miserable for all these years.

"Why would you risk his wrath again by helping me?" I asked.

"Because I want my life to end, and ending magic would end my curse."

I flipped my hair over my shoulder, but before I could ask any more questions, I heard a loud roar and felt the ground shake.

"What was that?" I asked.

With a swipe of her hand, the oasis disappeared, and we were back in the garden behind the cottage. We looked toward the sky and looming over us was a ghastly demon. He stood at least ten feet tall with tar-like skin and released the foulest smell. My nostrils burned whenever I inhaled, and his burning red eyes narrowed on my arm. It opened its black hole of a mouth and roared so loud I had to cover my ears. Mave grabbed my arm and hauled me back as the demon's spiked tail crashed down on the cottage and crushed it into dust.

Pieces of stone rained down as Mave yelled for me to get away. I ran as fast as I could past what was left of the house and down the cracked stone path. A scream made me falter, and I whirled around just as the demon flung Mave into a sharp slice of rock with one of its four stocky legs and turned on me. I ran as fast as my legs willed and hid behind a dilapidated wooden cottage, trying to catch my breath. The demon would see me pretty soon, but I needed to come up with a plan. And quick. The roar of the demon shook the ground, and I had to cover my ears again just to hear myself think. I caught a glimpse of the tattoo Sythion gave me out of the corner of my eye and how the demon seemed to home in on it. I leaned my head against the rotten wood and let out a soft groan as I figured out what the mark was doing. The stench of the demon was frighteningly close, and I stopped breathing as the demon roamed the area, looking for me.

The roof of the cottage creaked as the demon put a stumpy foot on it and sniffed. I peered up and clamped my eyes shut. It was right over me. If the demon deigned to look down, I would be nothing but ground beef. A cold, slimy substance hit my face, and I immediately gagged as I used my sleeve to wipe off the goop. I opened my eyes, only to find the demon staring straight at me. My muscles froze as its eyes roamed the area, looking for me, and I noticed that its red eyes were not eyes but, in fact, molten rock. I dared a step to my right and then another and another until I rounded the corner of the house. As soon as I was clear of its mouth, I sprinted back in the direction the demon threw Mave. The demon roared in frustration that it hadn't yet found its prey.

I found Mave slumped over a shard of stone, blood covering her face. I knelt and shook her gently, and when I heard her sigh, I shook her more forcefully, trying to wake her up.

"Mave, come on, I need your help."

She grumbled again, but didn't regain consciousness. I yelled, and that was my mistake. The demon turned on its heel toward the sound and charged. I stood up and braced myself for the assault. The demon's spiked tail whipped around and caught me right in the ribs. I howled in pain as I went airborne and crashed into what was left of the cobblestone wall.

My head went fuzzy and breathing was difficult. I looked down at my torso and found a large gash in my abdomen. Blood poured from the wound and I put my hand over it, trying to slow the bleeding. The demon roared again. If I didn't take a stand now, I was dead.

I stood up, my leg buckling underneath me. I tried once more, and I fell. The demon was getting ready to charge again, and I mustered all my strength and stood up, locking my knee.

My arm was covered in blood, and the black ink of the tattoo stood out against the bright red liquid. I clenched my jaw. I was the most powerful witch in my bloodline, and I would show Sythion that if he wanted to mess with me, it would be his last mistake.

I spread my feet apart and closed my eyes, concentrating on what I wanted to do. I opened my eyes and focused on the demon. Everything felt like it was going in slow motion. The demon's legs ran across houses and structures, crushing everything in its path, but I stayed focused on its rocky eyes.

I took a deep breath and let it out slowly as I flicked my wrist. The demon howled in pain as one of its legs twisted at an odd angle. I flicked my wrist again, and the demon went stumbling toward the ground as its other front leg broke. It slid to a stop in front of me and I flicked my wrist once more and heard its neck snap.

I slumped to the ground and crawled over to Mave. Her breathing was ragged and her skin was covered in yet more blood. I couldn't help her. I didn't know if I could help myself. Blood still spurted between my fingers from the wound on my abdomen. My breathing became labored and my eyesight was blurry. I was so tired. We won, and a nap sounded good. I slumped beside Mave and closed my eyes.

CHAPTER FIFTEEN

A FEW SECONDS LATER, I felt a pressure on my stomach. The ground was cold and hard, but I groaned, and I heard someone sigh. I couldn't open my eyes and tell them to go away. All I could do was moan in pain. My ears picked up on the distinct whoosh of a portal opening and then I felt the warmth of a soft surface. My body wanted to lean in to that sensation, and sleep, but I felt more pressure on my middle and a tugging sensation. I tried to swipe my hand at it and get it to go away, but my body wouldn't respond, so I just let the tugging continue and soon I fell into complete black.

I was once again in the mossy cave, and by this time, I had memorized details of the location. I noted the type of greenery around and the bubbling water nearby. It was a brook, or a stream, but definitely not a river. It was oddly peaceful, were it not for the reason I was here. I felt his presence before I heard him. My back stiffened, and I turned around to face Sythion.

"This tattoo... it draws demons to me, doesn't it?"

Sythion gave me a crooked smile. "The Curse of the Demon Rose. Whoever bears that mark"—he pointed to my arm—"shall draw demons to them wherever they go. You cannot escape it and you cannot break it. Cut the tattoo off and it will just appear on another part of the skin. I did warn you, Ebony, to stop trying to break the Seal, but you didn't listen."

I snorted. "Just like Mave didn't listen to you when she wanted to marry the man she loved? I'm starting to see a pattern here, Sythion. Someone does something you don't like, and you go berserk. Sounds an awful lot like you have some severe control issues."

Sythion chuckled. "You have a mouth on you, girl. I would be careful at whom you spew that attitude."

I put my hands on my hips. "Or what, you'll kill me?"

Sythion raised an eyebrow. "I can do far worse things than kill you, girl. I can make you kill yourself, or worse, kill the ones you love. That boy... Nightshade, was it? He's handsome for a Regelf. I'm sure you wouldn't want any harm to come to him. Or what about that human friend of yours, Sam? Melissa has told me all about him."

"You leave them out of this!" I charged at Sythion, but I ran straight through him, his form shimmering with the contact. I slid to a stop and whirled around, crossing my arms. "Really, an illusion? Are you that afraid of a sixteen-year-old girl?"

"It doesn't hurt to be prepared," he said.

I huffed and strode over to the stone well. Sythion cautiously followed me. What he had to be cautious about, I didn't know. This guy was the creator of all magic. The most powerful witch ever.

The shimmering gold of the pentagram seal reflected onto my skin, and I reached my hand to it. It felt like cool water, and when I withdrew my hand, there was a sheen of golden mist over my fingers.

"Fascinating it isn't it?" Sythion's voice was so close to me it made me shiver in disgust. I stepped back, and Sythion's form shimmered and dissipated. When he reconstituted, he was no longer Sythion. Richelle stood in front of me and her bright green eyes bore into me. I had long since come to terms with killing her, but maybe Sythion didn't know that. I let my jaw drop and I backed away a few paces, my eyes widening.

"Why are you doing this, Sythion?" I asked, "Why bring this memory back?"

"Am I just a memory to you?" Richelle asked. "Have you already forgotten what you did to me?"

Her form shifted. Her skin became paler and started decaying and her eyes glassed over, becoming cloudy. A sword appeared, protruding out of her gut and blood spilled from the wound.

"Am I just a memory now, Ebony? Remember how you killed me? Remember how it felt to have your blade slide through my flesh? Is that just a *memory*?"

I backed up until the cold, wet moss pressed against my back. Something sharp poked at me, and I wrapped my hand around a broken piece of rock. A plan formulated in my head, and I made my body shiver.

"Please, stop. I don't want to see this," I mumbled.

"You did this to me, Ebony." Richelle took a step toward me, and another. "You can't escape that you're a cold-blooded murderer."

She took another step, and that was when I stilled my body and smiled viciously. "I wonder, Sythion, if you can actually read my memories, or if you're just fantastic at deceiving people."

Richelle's face contorted in confusion and I pulled the shard of rock off the stone wall and plunged it into her heart.

And hopefully, Sythion's.

The shard went straight through Richelle's form with no resistance. Right. This was an illusion. Richelle's rotting corpse laughed, and the sound got deeper as Sythion appeared once more.

"I have to say, girl, that was clever, but not clever enough."

Sythion raised his hand and flicked two fingers toward the ground, and gravity hit me like a ton of bricks. I struggled to stay upright, but it was like fighting against the weight of seven elephants. My knees buckled and Sythion chuckled.

"You know you're not the only one looking to break the seal."

The gravity knocked the breath out of me, but I gasped out, "Then why not go harass them?"

Sythion pulled on his beard thoughtfully. "Because if anyone is likely to actually pull it off, it would be you."

My arms shook under the unbearable weight. My bones felt like they were being compressed to the point of shattering.

Sythion squatted in front of me and looked me in the eye. "I will tell you this though and think of it as my gift to you. Be careful who you trust. Not everyone is as... forgiving as I am."

Lifting my head was a struggle, but I managed to look Sythion right in deep green eyes. "You call this forgiving?"

Sythion's eyes flashed with sadness, just like the last time we met, but it was gone in an instant, replaced with fury.

Sythion flicked his fingers toward the ground again and the weight became even heavier. I fought against it as best I could, but my arms couldn't take any more. They gave out, and my head slammed against the stone floor of the cave, and I blacked out.

Steady hands caught me as I jolted upright. The movement caused me to flinch from the pain, and Nightshade shushed me.

"How are you feeling?" he asked.

I flexed my muscles and tested my body. "Sore, my gut hurts, and Sythion invaded my dreams again, but other than that I feel like a million bucks."

Nightshade's eyebrows knit together. "You saw Sythion?"

I nodded. "Although he didn't look like Sythion for very long. He morphed into Richelle's corpse and that was about the creepiest thing I had ever seen."

"I am so sorry. That must have been horrible for you. I know it still haunts you that you killed her."

Nightshade still cared about me, I realized. He cared about how I felt, and after spending time apart from him, I also realized he didn't quite get me as much as I thought he did. I still loved him, though, and my heart ached every time I thought about him. I reached my hand out, and he grabbed it. Whether instinctively or not, I didn't know, and frankly, I didn't care. All I knew was it felt like home when we were touching. His thumb caressed the back of my hand and I barely noticed when the door to the infirmary opened.

Peyton walked into the room and halted when he saw us. I jerked apart from Nightshade, and he looked between me and Peyton with a scowl on his face. Without another word, he marched out of the infirmary. Peyton smirked as he passed, and I shot Peyton a dirty look. He shrugged as he sauntered to me and took Nightshade's place on the edge of my bed.

"Jealous, isn't he?"

I smacked Peyton's arm. "Be nice. The breakup was hard on both of us."

"Seems to be harder on him than he wants to admit," he said.

I snorted. "Sounds like you're jealous,"

"I am."

My heart skipped a beat. "What?"

His icy blue eyes focused on mine. "I am jealous. I'm jealous that you were his first love. And that you loved him back just as fiercely. I'm jealous because every time I'm around you, I'm wondering if you still think about him. And every time I'm around you, I can't think of anything besides you and there way your hair is almost golden brown in the light, the way your eyes sparkle with mischief, and the way you would do anything for the people you love, and I always wonder in the back of my mind if you think the same things about him. And it kills me to think of that."

My breathing hitched, and I swore he could hear my heart going a hundred miles an hour. "I still love Nightshade, but I haven't thought about him much since the breakup. I think... I think I was trying to hide from the pain, but in doing that, I think I'm able to... not exactly move on, but move forward. And I found something I hadn't even been looking for. In you."

Peyton's face inched closer to mine, his eyes now darting between my lips and my eyes. "And what is it you found?" His voice was barely a whisper.

"Someone who challenges me and pushes me to be my best, even when I don't want to be. Someone who isn't afraid to match my attitude and someone who will call me on my crap because they know I can be immature sometimes. I found all that and more in you, Peyton."

Peyton's face was a mere millimeter from my own. "Ebony."

He said my name like a caress as our lips met, and a thousand stars exploded in me all at once. I gasped and pulled him closer. He moaned into my mouth as he wrapped his hand gingerly around my waist, taking care of my wound, and gently pressed me closer to him. I deepened the kiss, and his arm tightened around me slightly.

When we broke apart, we were both breathing heavily, and he caressed my cheek with the back of his hand.

"I've wanted to do that for a while," he said.

I smiled. "You can do it again if you want."

His lips met mine once more, and his hands explored my body. He caressed my arms, my waist, and everywhere he touched me made me shiver, but it wasn't the same. I broke the kiss, and Peyton knit his eyebrows together.

"Did I do something wrong?" he asked.

I shook my head. "I just... I can't."

Peyton bit his lip. "You wanted it to be him."

I nodded and looked down at my hands knotting in the sheet, unable to stand seeing the hurt in his eyes. I felt Peyton get off the bed. My chest heaved when he left the room, and I flopped back on the pillow and sobbed until I fell into a restless sleep.

CHAPTER SIXTEEN

T HE NEXT MORNING, I was sitting up in bed, drinking some health tonic that the healer left for me, when Dad and Uncle Hesperus walked through the open double doors. Evan and Valerie strolled in behind them, and Evan's face showed his surprise that I was still alive. I had to remember to slap him at some point.

"How are you feeling?" Dad asked.

I tested my muscles and groaned. "Could be better. How's Mave?"

Uncle Hesperus sat on the edge of my bed and put his hand on my knee. "She's... alive. She's in a coma and her face is pretty bashed up, but she's breathing."

My muscles relaxed at the news. I didn't know why, but I had expected Mave to be dead from that throw. And she should have been, but thanks to Sythion and his curse, she was immortal.

Even so, would she heal?

I tried to get out of bed, but my gut protested, and spots danced across my eyes. I lay back down and tried to catch my breath. Uncle Hesperus shushed me and smoothed the covers over my body.

"You're still healing. That demon did a number on you."

"It would have been worse if I hadn't killed that thing when I did."

"How *did* you kill it?" Evan asked, crossing his arms. "I mean, I saw how big that thing was. It could have eaten you in one bite."

"Not that it's any of your concern, but Mave taught me a few new tricks."

"What kind of tricks?" Dad asked.

I shrugged. "How to do magic without spells."

Dad's face went ashen, and Uncle Hesperus pursed his lips.

"What?" I asked.

"That's a dangerous way to do magic." Uncle Hesperus said. "Did she also give you that mark on your arm? Is it to help with the spells?"

I looked at my left arm and quickly put it under the covers. "No. Actually Sythion gave me this. He called it the Curse of the Demon Rose. It draws demons to me."

Valerie scooted closer to Evan, and he put his arm around her waist. Gross. I would have to have a serious talk with her about trusting Evan with anything, especially her heart.

"We'll have to keep you somewhere safe, then." Dad's voice was hard, but there was something underneath his tone.

"No! I have to see this through. People are counting on me. Besides, if we end magic, then the curse doesn't matter anymore. There would be no more demons to attack me."

Nightshade burst into the infirmary with a dozen guards. "The rioters broke through the gate. We have to get you all to a safe place. Now."

My heart jumped, and it wasn't because of the news. Nightshade always had that effect on me, despite whatever danger we faced. Uncle Hesperus and Dad promptly went into action. They helped me off the bed and carried most of my weight as we ran out of the infirmary to the safe house.

The safe house was on the outskirts of the castle, just past the walls, and it housed enough rations where our whole family could survive for weeks if necessary. We took the stairs down to the lower level and ran past the doors to the garden. Peyton was there with another guard, waiting to escort us out through a small door at the end of the corridor. We rushed through the underground tunnel, slowly ascending, and another set of guards waited at the other end to open a set of enchanted double doors. The doors creaked loudly as they swung open, as if no one had used them in decades. We all filed in, the guards first, and they opened another set of double doors. These belonged to a wooden wardrobe that led into the safe house.

The fireplace was already roaring in the corner, although it seemed like its purpose was to make the place cozier rather than to heat the house. The living area was spacious, but there were about a dozen guards surrounding us, so the space became cramped very quickly.

I sat in a big armchair next to the fireplace and warmed my hands. Peyton sat on the floor in front of me. I noticed Nightshade from the corner of my eye, and the look on his face was similar to how Sam looked at me at Melissa's funeral. It was a mix of hurt and fury. I shook that thought out of my head. I couldn't afford to think about that right now. Not when I had so much to worry about already.

Dad walked up behind me and put his hands on the back of the chair. "You're still hurt. You should get some rest. I had one of the guards make a room for you."

I shook my head. "What are we even doing in here? We should be out there helping those people. *Our* people. They hate us enough already, and now we're sequestered in a bunker while they're trying to tell us how much pain they're in. It doesn't seem fair to me."

"It's not," Peyton said.

"But it is necessary," Nightshade countered. "You are right, Ebony. They are in pain and they are scared, and fear makes people do things they would not normally do."

"You would know," Peyton muttered.

Nightshade whirled on Peyton, his voice menacing and cold. "What are you insinuating?"

"Just that if you weren't terrified Ebony would leave your sorry ass for someone better, like me, you wouldn't have left first."

"Peyton," I warned.

Peyton shrugged. "I'm just telling him what he already knows."

Nightshade straightened his back and narrowed his eyes. "I left because it was clear she did not love me the way I loved her."

"That's not true!" I rose from the chair, and my vision went black as my body swayed.

Peyton helped me sit back down and covered me with a wool blanket hanging over the back of the seat. I shivered from the change in temperature, and Peyton wrapped the blanket tighter around me. Nightshade scoffed and stalked off. I wanted to go after him. I wanted to talk to him and explain that I would always love him, but I didn't have the strength.

"You need to get some rest." Peyton said.

I nodded, and Peyton helped me out of the chair. A knock sounded at the front door, and the guards immediately went on alert. No one was supposed to know we were here. The knocking turned to pounding, and the wood splintered in every direction as someone busted the door down. The dust settled and Warwick stood in the open doorway, Sam and Delilah behind him.

"Warwick?" I asked. "What's going on?"

His eyes were anything but kind when they met my gaze.

"Sorry Princess," he said, "you're coming with us."

The guards went on the offensive, but Warwick thrust out his hand and shouted, "*Ruina*!"

Every guard in the room collapsed.

I balled my hands into fists, though I wasn't strong enough to punch him. "What did you do to them?"

"He put them to sleep," Sam said. "Don't worry. He's not a murderer like you."

"Sam..."

"Don't you dare talk to him," Delilah said. "Warwick, bring them, *all* of them."

Peyton jumped up and thrust his hands out, ready to cast magic, but I shed the blanket and put my hand on his forearm. He looked at me in disbelief, but I shook my head, indicating that he should stand down. I limped toward Warwick, but I didn't meet his eyes. Instead, I looked at Sam with as much malice as I could muster as my family and I strode past him.

Warwick's band of bandits led us past the crowd of rioters, Sam and Delilah in tow. We passed buildings and storefronts being looted, while people of all races and species held torches and lit piles of books and supplies on fire. My vision was going blurry as I walked, but Warwick led me by the elbow and held most of my weight as we trudged toward the center of the city.

"Where are we going?" My voice sounded like I was underwater.

"You and your family are being put on trial for your crimes against the realm."

"Crimes?"

"You're still so clueless," Evan said, walking alongside Sam as if they had been best friends for years. "Have you even asked yourself where all the money your family has comes from? It's not just from taxes."

I halted and crossed my arms. "Well, since you seem to know so much, where do we get all the money?"

"From a pool," Peyton muttered sadly.

"From a what?"

"A pool. Everyone puts money into this vast vault for the royal family. It pays for the palace staff, the crown jewels, and things like that."

My jaw dropped as I turned toward my uncle. "We take money from our people to pay for our lifestyle?"

Uncle Hesperus ran his fingers through his long hair as he sighed. "Yes."

"Why haven't you abolished that practice?"

"Because he's the one who enforced the pool in the first place," Warwick said.

I looked at my uncle through new eyes. Our people were suffering, and my family took money from their livelihoods to pay for our opulence. I turned away in shame and started walking toward the city square. We deserved to be put on trial for this.

We reached the center of the city, and in the square, there was a makeshift courtroom set up. Three chairs were sitting on a dais, and there was a large crowd milling about. My family and I took our places on the dais and the crowd started yelling. Evan stepped in front of us and silenced them. Warwick, Valerie, Sam, and Delilah stood to the side, and I wondered how they knew Evan and what their place in the trial was. Two bandits escorted Peyton and Nightshade to the front of the crowd, facing us. A front-row seat. Their faces were grim as the trail began.

CHAPTER SEVENTEEN

THE TRIAL STARTED INNOCENTLY enough, with Evan listing off several things that my family had that our people paid for out of the pool. But then it took a turn.

"Ebony Amberwood," Evan shouted. "It is not only your family that is on trial for the mishandling of people's income, but you yourself are on trial for the destruction of not only Amethystia, but the human realm as well. How do you plead?"

My mouth dropped open with an audible pop. "I don't know what you're talking about."

"You know exactly what he's talking about!" Delilah stepped forward and turned toward the crowd as she pointed a finger at me. "This girl has repeatedly undermined both of our worlds. I may be human, but injustice is injustice no matter who, or what, we all are. I demand justice for my father, who was killed thanks to this... *traitor's* actions. If any of you have had a loved one die because of her negligence, then stand with me as we bring her to justice!"

The crowd yelled their agreement and Evan looked slightly annoyed that a mere human took his spotlight away. Valerie shrunk back at the noise and wrapped her arms around herself. To her credit, she looked very uncomfortable with the accusations being thrown at me. Peyton and Nightshade both tensed, and they were about to hurl themselves in front of me.

I took a deep breath and straightened my back. "I am no traitor! I have been busting my ass trying to stop all of this."

"But have you succeeded?" Evan said.

I was about to bark a retort, but something in me stopped short. I haven't succeeded in my mission and telling everyone I had a plan would just give them more ammunition against me if I failed. Delilah raised an eyebrow. She knew I didn't have a good defense, and she was going to take advantage of it.

She turned to the crowd once more. "See? She even lies about stopping all this craziness! We need to stop *her* before she destroys even more lives! Who's with me?"

The crowd cheered. My heart rate picked up. This was not good.

Evan stood by Delilah and put his hand on her shoulder. "Witches and humans, working side by side. That is what's needed to stop the menace that is Ebony Amberwood. I say she's guilty. What's your verdict?"

He looked at Delilah, and a wicked gleam shone in her eye. It reminded me so much of the way Fabian used to look at me.

"Guilty," She said.

The crowd cheered louder, and Nightshade tried to bust through and get to me, but one of Warwick's bandits grabbed him by the shoulder and pulled him to a stop.

"Ebony!" Nightshade tried to get to me again, but a swift punch to the gut from the bandit had him on his knees.

"Nightshade!" I jumped up from the chair, and Warwick rushed me.

He tackled me to the ground, and warmth trickled down my cheek as my face slammed into the rough wood of the makeshift dais.

Evan and Delilah, by some miracle, got the crowd settled down, and they both turned to me.

Evan gave me a wicked smile. "Ebony Amberwood, the people of Amethystia have found you guilty of treason. Normally, the sentence for this is death, but I think it would be more fitting to treat you like the criminal you have always been. So it is with a heavy heart that I hereby exile you from this realm."

The crowd was hysterical. Some yelling their triumph, while others shouting exile wasn't harsh enough. Warwick helped me off the ground, and I caught Sam's eye. He glanced down, and I thought it was weird that he had been quiet throughout this entire ordeal. Evan stepped up onto the dais and opened a portal.

He bent down and whispered, "Good luck being hunted down in both worlds." Then he shoved me through the swirling vortex.

I found myself on Essex Street, my palms scraping the pavement as I landed on my hands and knees. I brushed myself off and bit back the tears as I headed back to Aunt Jasmine's house. Only when I got there, someone had burned it to the ground. Embers still shone through the smoke as I took in the destruction. Screeches brought my attention to the sky. Flying demons circled overhead.

These demons, however, differed from the ones back at Mave's. They were bright red, and their wings were almost transparent. I could see every vein going through the thin skin. Their beaks looked more ferocious, too. It almost looked like a pterodactyl mixed with a toucan. I took one last look at the now nonexistent house and ran to find cover.

Every building I found that was still standing had either been overrun by the hundreds of demons now roaming the streets or had been taken over by humans trying to survive. I thought about lying and saying I was human too, but if I was ever discovered, I would be in more danger. So I wandered the town, the gash on my side throbbing, and ended up in front of a two-story house that had mostly survived the demon attacks. I vaguely wondered if Melissa's dad was still inhabiting the house, or if he had sense enough to leave. The other possibility snaked through my thoughts as I snuck in through the front door and closed it as stealthily as I could, but I promptly shoved the thought out. I didn't know if anyone was in the house, but if they were, I didn't want to alert them to my presence.

I tiptoed around the first floor looking for anyone, or anything, that might be lurking. A fine layer of dust covered the furniture, as if no one had been here for months, and the electricity didn't work. I made my way upstairs, and as I did, I heard a rustling coming from a bedroom off to the right. I stopped short and strained my ears. The rustling sounded again, and I readied my hands to cast magic. I tried to not make any noise as I reached the room and flung open the door. A blast of magic hurtled toward me, but with a flick of my wrist, it fizzled out before it could hit me in the face. A woman with tangled brown hair and dirt all over her face blinked at me.

"Aunt Jasmine?"

"Ebony!" She rushed toward me and pulled me into the biggest hug I had ever received. "I thought you were in Amethystia."

I pulled out of the hug and rubbed my arms. "I was, but... I can't go back there anymore."

"What happened?"

I shook my head, unable to say the words because if I did, I might just start crying. Aunt Jasmine noticed and brushed my hair out of my face. We said nothing as we made our way back downstairs and sat on the couch. The lack of air circulation made it stuffy inside, but it wasn't overly uncomfortable. I thought about what had happened today, and my body suddenly grew weary. I wanted to take a nap right then and there, but I knew I had to fill Aunt Jasmine in on the situation back home.

We sat in the dark while I recounted the events leading up to me coming here. Aunt Jasmine looked appalled, but not surprised. Apparently, the witches who helped Sam and Delilah had made a deal with them. They would help hunt down their own kind if the witch hunters would help them take down our family. That explained why Sam and Delilah were in Amethystia in the first place. I wondered how they knew where the safe house was, given that no one was supposed to know its location, but I put that thought to the side as I yawned.

Aunt Jasmine looked like she had more to tell me and when I prompted, she shook her head and told me to not worry about it until after I had slept. I decided she was right, and that my body needed the rest, but when I went upstairs, I froze. I couldn't go into Melissa's room. Even after all these months, I wasn't ready to face that. So, I went back downstairs and pulled a blanket out of a closet and curled up on the couch.

CHAPTER EIGHTEEN

THE NEXT MORNING, THE smell of smoke woke me, and I ventured out to the backyard where Aunt Jasmine had a small fire going. I raised an eyebrow at the sight, but she said nothing as she handed me a bowl of baked beans. The only thing she could muster up in the kitchen, no doubt. I sat beside her and started digging in. We stayed silent long enough that the fire died down, and when it was nothing more than embers crackling in a pile of ashes, I finally spoke.

"What happened to your house?"

"Demons. What happened to your cheek?"

"Long story."

Aunt Jasmine's mouth turned up at the corner. "I'm listening."

I recounted everything from unrest at the gates to the trial and my second exile from Amethystia. When I was done, Aunt Jasmine's leg was bouncing up and down as she played with her tangled hair.

"Your uncle has gotten our family into way more messes than he cares to admit, but I don't like the idea of the people using his crimes to punish you even further."

I stood up and dusted off my pants. "I don't think it was the people, exactly. It seems to me a few loud mouths have the attention of the masses."

I thought back to Evan and Delilah, and I couldn't shake the feeling that something wasn't adding up with them.

Aunt Jasmine chewed her lip. "That can be dangerous for several reasons."

"I need to get back to Amethystia," I said. "I have to find that well and end all of this. For good."

Aunt Jasmine stood up and brushed dirt over the ashes for good measure. The last thing we wanted was for a group of demons or witch hunters to see the smoke.

"I'll help you. Whatever you need," Aunt Jasmine said.

I hugged her fiercely. She hugged me back with just as much force. When we let go, Aunt Jasmine had tears in her eyes.

"I promise I will fix things," I said, "but what I need from you is going to be dangerous. I need you to go to Amethystia and find Sam because I think I need to talk to him."

"No," Aunt Jasmine said.

My eyebrows knit together. "Why not?"

"Because I already found him."

She pointed behind me and I reluctantly turned around. Sam was standing by the back fence with his hands in his pockets, looking everywhere but at me.

"Hi," I said warily.

Why was he here?

He nodded a greeting. I glanced at Aunt Jasmine, and she gave my shoulder a slight squeeze before heading back inside to give us some privacy.

"What are you doing here?" I asked.

"Looking for you. What are you doing here?"

I knew he didn't mean in general. "I couldn't find another place to go. Our house—"

"I saw. I'm sorry."

"Me too."

Awkward silence grew between us, and I couldn't think of anything to say. I didn't have to say anything, however, because Sam said it all for me.

"I am by no means saying we're friends again, but I think we have the same goal. I heard your family talking about how you were trying to find some siphon or something to end magic—"

"Sythion," I interrupted.

"Huh?"

"I'm trying to find the Seal of Sythion. It's a magical seal on a well that houses all magic. Break that seal, and we can stop all of this. The demons, the deaths, the fighting. Everything."

Sam nodded. "I want to help. More than that, I think you *need* my help."

"I think we need each other's help."

Sam took his hands out of his pockets and finally looked me in the eye with grim determination. "I propose a truce. We find this well and when it's all over, we never see each other again."

"Why should I trust you? You killed my mother. *In front of me.* What's to say you won't do that to me, too?"

"What's to say you won't kill me in my sleep? We both have done terrible things Ebony. I'm not saying this truce will be a perfect one, or even a comfortable one, but you need help to get back to your realm and finding this thing, and I need help to end magic, and Delilah doesn't seem at all interested in that. Are you in or not?"

I clenched and unclenched my jaw several times before nodding once and turning to head inside without checking if Sam followed.

Once inside, I sat on the couch next to Aunt Jasmine, and Sam sat opposite us. To his credit, he looked very uncomfortable when Aunt Jasmine stared him down. We sat in silence for what seemed like forever, but when I could no longer take it, I cleared my throat.

"Sam is going to help me find the Seal of Sythion."

"Is he? Or is he just going to tie you to a stake again and watch *you* burn this time?" Aunt Jasmine's eyes never left Sam's, and every time Sam tried to look away, she raised an eyebrow. I swallowed.

"I understand you're still upset, Aunt Jasmine, but—"

"Upset that he killed my sister in cold blood? Why on earth would I be upset about that?"

"*But*," I continued, "with his help, we'll be able to end all of this a lot sooner than if I was by myself. Besides, I don't know of a way to get back home without alerting everyone, and I think Sam can help with that."

"How?" Aunt Jasmine crossed her arms.

"My girlfriend," Sam said. "She has friends who are witches. They... they hate your family and will do anything to overthrow you guys."

Aunt Jasmine raised a brow. "You mean like killing their own kind?"

"Yeah," Sam's voice trembled just a bit, like if he said the wrong thing, Aunt Jasmine would annihilate him. "They owe me a favor. I can get them to portal us into a secluded part of the realm. Just tell me where that is, and I'll get us there."

I crossed my legs. "We'll need to be close to the Elder Woods."

"I thought the woods were a myth," Aunt Jasmine mused.

"Apparently not. I can feel the magic, even from here. It's... part of my new ability to cast without spells."

"You have a new ability?" Sam asked, his eyes wary.

I sat up straighter and smiled smugly. "Don't worry. I won't turn you into a rat, even though that's what you deserve."

Sam rolled his eyes and rose from his seat. "We need to get going, then."

I stood as well and nodded, but Aunt Jasmine stayed seated.

"What's wrong?" I asked.

Aunt Jasmine met my eyes, and tears shone from the light coming through the window. "Be careful. I can't lose you too."

I wrapped her in a hug, and she squeezed me back tightly. When we broke apart, both of us had tears in our eyes.

"I love you," I said, and Sam and I were off to go end all this once and for all.

We waited by the high school gym entrance for his two witch friends. I bounced on my toes and looked around for anything out of the ordinary. I heard a whooshing sound and a portal, a sphere of swirling rainbows, opened and out stepped a tall man and an even taller woman. The man looked to be in his forties with his hair already graying at the sides, and the woman looked twenty years younger than him, with glowing skin and red hair so bright it made me want to squint. When they saw me, their eyebrows rose.

"Getting soft on us, Freeman?" the woman said with a sneer. "Should we go tell Delilah that her little boy toy misses his friend and wants to go back to her?"

Sam rolled his eyes. "Shut up Zena. Just open a portal for us and *don't* tell Delilah, and we'll be even."

The man stroked his well-trimmed beard. "I don't think so. This isn't like when we brought that human girl, Victoria or what's her name, to Amethystia."

"*You* brought her to Amethystia?" No wonder she hesitated when I asked how she had gotten there.

"Yeah, but I think the stakes have now been raised, and we want payment. Up front."

I crossed my arms and huffed. "And what payment would that be, exactly?"

Sam elbowed me in the ribs and told me to shut up, but I didn't like the looks of these two. They oozed arrogance, and I wanted to take them down a couple of pegs.

They smirked at each other and before I could even process what was happening, the woman thrust a fireball at me.

I yelled as I ducked, but not before the fire scorched my hair. I tried to put it out, and the two witches laughed when Sam had to cover my head with his jacket.

"What the hell, Zena!" Sam yelled. "We had a deal."

"The deal was to get the two of you back to Amethystia without telling Delilah. There was never anything said about not hurting her before we do."

The man smiled cruelly as he said, "*Electricae sphaera!*"

A sphere of crackling electricity formed in his hand. I dropped the jacket as Sam and I took cover behind the steel door that led into the school.

"Nice plan," I said as the man thrust the ball of lightning at the door.

"It would have worked if you and your family weren't such monsters," Sam shot back.

"Hey, I had no idea what my family was doing, and if I did, I would have stopped it."

"I know."

"You—what?" I forgot all about the magic projectiles being thrown at us and how hot the metal was getting.

Sam sighed. "You're a lot of things, Ebony, but you wouldn't take from people who have nothing."

I couldn't even reply because the door was turning red. The metal scorched my skin, and Sam and I took a chance and ran inside the gym. I stopped dead in my tracks at what I saw.

The remains of my mother still clung to the wooden post that they erected. I sank to my knees and my breath was shallow and ragged. When the two witches caught up to us, they also halted.

"Whoa," the man said, "that's...messed up."

I laughed through the tears that were gradually making their way down my cheeks. "Didn't you guys help do this?"

The woman, Zena, shook her head. "We knew Delilah was hunting witches, but the two of us never agreed with it."

"We stayed away from all that stuff. Too gruesome and cruel," the man agreed.

Zena knelt by me and put her hand on my shoulder. "Who was that?"

I sniffled. "My mother."

Zena swore.

I nodded. "They made me watch. I couldn't do anything. I tried to escape. I tried screaming for help. No one came. At least no one came in time. Her screams still haunt my nightmares."

"Mine too." Sam's voice was sad, almost regretful.

I whipped my head toward him. "You did this. Why? Because of Melissa? Melissa wasn't my fault. Fabian killed her. I couldn't do anything. I was in a cell, remember? If you two hadn't tried to play hero—"

"I know!" Sam's voice cracked, and he swallowed hard before continuing. "You think I don't know whose fault it is? It's mine. I was the one who told her we had to rescue you that day. She told me no. That we had to go get someone who could actually help. She was scared out of her mind, but I didn't give a damn, and now she's dead."

Tears stained his cheeks as sobs took over his body. The two witches were watching our exchange like a tennis match, but said nothing.

"Then why put the blame on me?"

Sam laughed without humor and ran his hand roughly through his hair. "Don't you get it, Ebony? I hate myself for what happened. I couldn't, still can't, look at myself in the mirror. Blaming you seemed easier than to live with what I did. What I'm still doing."

I stood up and trudged over to Sam. I didn't even think twice as I wrapped him in a big hug and, after a few seconds of hesitation, he hugged me back, tightening his grip around my waist until I could barely breathe.

I didn't know how long we stayed like that, but when we broke apart, Sam sniffled and gave me a little smile. This didn't fix anything between us, but it made our truce that much stronger.

"Let's go end this," I sighed.

Sam nodded, and we turned toward the two witches. The man opened a portal without a word, and we all stepped through.

CHAPTER NINETEEN

THE SMELL OF DAMP earth and moss greeted us as we stepped through the other side of the portal. The trees were so dense, I couldn't see through them. I could feel the magic there, though, and it almost made me double over in shock. We were definitely in the right place. Sam and the others looked around them.

"Where are we?" Sam asked.

I knit my eyebrows together. "The Elder Woods."

Sam raised an eyebrow at me. "We're in the middle of a field."

I looked at the others, and they told me the same thing. The magic was so strong, but I wondered if I was the only one who could feel it, if I was the only one who could see where we were. The two witches shrugged at each other and stepped back through the portal, leaving me and Sam alone. I grabbed his hand and tugged him over to where I was standing.

"Do you feel anything?" I asked.

Sam paced, looking around. "What am I supposed to be feeling?"

I sighed. How were we supposed to find the Seal if Sam couldn't even see where we were headed? An idea popped into my head. I stood behind Sam and squeezed his shoulders.

"What are you—"

"Shh," I commanded.

I closed my eyes and envisioned The Elder Woods just as I saw them. I then envisioned Sam seeing what I was. My hands felt warm, and when I peeked through my long lashes, light leaked between my fingers.

I opened my eyes and told Sam to do the same. When he did, he gasped and looked all around him. My features twisted into an expression of triumph as I saw the wonder in Sam's eyes. It all turned dark, however, when he glared at me.

"Never use magic on me again."

I huffed. Of course, that would be his takeaway. I shoved past him and looked over my shoulder.

"If we're going to be working together, we need to be seeing the same things."

He didn't answer as he followed me into the thicket of trees. We went as far as we could, but the brush was too thick for us to go any further and neither of us had brought any weapons.

"What now, oh so *powerful* genius?" Sam asked.

Powerful... I could use that. I slid him a sly smile and swung my right arm out to the side. Glittering lights floated in the air around my hand and Phantomseeker, the Delacroix family sword, *my* family sword appeared in my palm.

Sam rolled his eyes as I hacked my way through the brush and thorns with no problems. We stopped to rest when the light all but disappeared. We were both covered in sweat and desperately needed some water, but somehow we kept the bickering to a minimum. Sam pointed to some smoke billowing in the distance, and we took our chances of creeping towards it.

We found a tiny cabin about half a mile from where we rested, and before I even knocked on the door, an elf with dark gray skin and bloodred eyes opened the dilapidated wooden door and raised a thinly arched eyebrow.

"And what do we have here?" His voice was like honey, soft and warm, and I wanted to sink into it. "Two witches, all alone in these woods, where anything can happen to them?"

"One witch," Sam corrected.

"Excuse me?" the elf said, his pointed ears twitching slightly.

"One witch," Sam repeated. "I'm human."

"Oh." The elf's voice changed. It was now more gravely and sounded like he had been a longtime smoker. "That changes things. You two look very thirsty. Come in and I'll give you some fresh water."

We stepped through the door, and I did a double take. The interior of the home was well furnished and not a speck of dust was anywhere inside. The walls weren't even logs, they looked like marble.

"How..." I trailed off as a shimmer of the real cabin peeked through the illusion. I put my hands on my hips and raised a brow at the elf and he shrugged as he walked past us towards the kitchen.

"So I like to do interior design. Sue me."

I shook my head as Sam and I sat down at the lavish mahogany table. Once again, the illusion shimmered, and I saw a glimpse of the actual table we sat at. The wood was rotten and bugs of all kinds crawled along the surface. And then the lavish table returned. I tried not to gag as the elf set two golden goblets down in front of us. I could only imagine the real cups we were about to sip from.

"So what brings a witch and a... human all the way into the Elder Woods?" the elf asked as he sat at the head of the table.

"We're looking for the Seal of Sythion." Sam said.

I kicked him underneath the table, and he winced. Good. The elf's eyes darkened.

"And what do you want with it?" His voice had gone icy.

"We want to end magic," Sam again answered, and I wanted to do more than kick him.

"Do you now?"

Sam nodded once, and the elf laughed. "Well, I'll be damned if that isn't the funniest thing I've ever heard. A witch, a powerful one at that — I could smell you coming a mile away — and a human want to end magic. What a delight!"

Neither Sam nor I laughed, and the elf stopped his giggles. "Oh, you were being serious. Well, I must say that in my hundreds of years in this realm, I have never heard of a more ridiculous quest."

"Why?" I asked.

"Because it's a fool's errand. Not only would Sythion not be absentminded enough to just leave the seal for anyone to find, but he wouldn't make it so easy to destroy it either... wait." He looked at Sam through narrowed eyes. "You said you were human?"

Sam nodded once more. The elf stroked his chin.

"There might be some hope for you two yet."

"Why does the fact that Sam's a human matter?" I lifted my chin.

"Because only a human can destroy the Seal." He stated that fact like we were discussing the weather.

"None of the books we read mentioned that."

The elf laughed once. "Well, why would they? No one wants the seal destroyed. We all like having magic."

"Some of us don't," I muttered and my mind went to Mave, who was still in a coma in the palace infirmary.

"Who? You and your little pet? Please, we'd all be better off dead than without our magic."

"I am no one's pet," Sam growled.

The elf just smirked. "You certainly bark like one."

Sam scowled, and I cleared my throat before one of them decided to bite. "We should get going. Thank you for the hospitality. It means a lot."

Before I could even blink though, invisible bonds wrapped around me, and given Sam's struggling, the same was being done to him.

"Oh, I don't think so," the elf said, his voice once again like honey. "I see that mark on your wrist and it's... calling to me. The Curse of the Demon Rose, correct? You've already encountered my lord Sythion then. Well, let me introduce myself. I am Merlok."

I tried to calm my struggling enough to think. I remembered reading about Merlok and various others when we were researching Sythion's Seal. They were Sythion's followers who worshiped him like a god. And we just told one of them our plan to destroy the one thing they hold dear. This wasn't going to end well.

CHAPTER TWENTY

MERLOK DRAGGED ME AND Sam into the living room and shoved each of us into a different corner. Its marble walls melted into the dilapidated cabin we saw from outside. He heaved us onto the floor and bugs of every shape and size started crawling all over us. Every instinct in my body wanted to gag and shake them off, but I knew Merlok was waiting for that sort of reaction. That he would take pleasure from it. So instead, I let the bugs slither over me and gave Merlok a death glare.

"What's the matter?" Merlok mocked. "Are my friends a little *too* friendly? And here I thought you would have liked them since you like to keep... vermin as company." He slid his eyes over to Sam.

"Screw you!" Sam shouted.

"Tsk tsk tsk." Merlok shook his finger at me. "You should teach your pet manners. They really do go a long way."

I spit at him and hit him in the face. "In this instance, I actually agree with him."

Merlok jumped back and wiped his cheek. "That wasn't nice." He kicked me in the stomach and all the breath rushed out of my lungs.

"Don't touch her!" Sam said.

Merlok looked between us and laughed maniacally. "That's adorable! A witch and her human pet together!"

Sam looked away, and Merlok gasped. "Or not together, but the human vermin wants to be. This just keeps getting better and better."

My eyes grew wide as they shot to Sam. He stared Merlok down with murderous intent.

I growled at Merlok, and he just laughed again. "Oh, don't worry, my little witch. We'll have some fun too. However, since you need a human to destroy the Seal, I think I'll carve up your pet first."

"My name is Sam, and you best remember that, since I'm going to be the one to kill you."

Merlok sauntered over to Sam and grabbed him by the hair. Sam let out a yelp, and Merlok smashed his head into the rotting wood wall. Blood gushed from a wound on his forehead. Sam thrashed and fought as Merlok smashed his head into the wall again and again.

"Stop!" I yelled. "He's had enough. Just stop."

Merlok let Sam go, and he crumpled into a heap. His chest rose and fell in shallow breaths, and I silently thanked Hecate that he was alright.

Merlok bent over me and pulled me up by my elbow. "I'll say when your little vermin of a lover has had enough. You get to sit there like a good little witch and watch as I destroy him. Just like you were going to destroy something that was precious to me."

"I'm still going to destroy that seal. If it's the last thing I do," I spat.

Merlok shoved his face into mine, and I smelled the rot in his breath. "Over my corpse."

I gagged, and his features twisted into a scowl. He threw me against the wall and I slid onto my butt. I looked over at Sam, who had bugs covering every inch of his body, but he was still breathing.

Merlok grabbed a cloak from the hook by the door and gave us one last look before telling us not to move as he shoved his way outside. When I heard his footsteps fade, I scooted my way over to Sam and brushed the bugs off him the best I could while still in invisible bonds. He stirred, and I helped him sit up with my body.

"Are you okay?" I asked.

He nodded feebly.

"Good, we need a plan."

"Use... your sword." Sam's voice was weak and there was a small pool of blood on the floor where he had been lying. I silently cursed whatever powers were out to get me. Sam couldn't fight in his condition.

"I can't. These bonds... they're stopping me from using my magic."

Sam scooted closer to me. "Back pocket."

I saw a small shape sticking out of the pocket. I scooted around so we were back-to-back, and I used my hands to grab a metal object out of the pocket of his jeans. It dropped to the ground with a small clang, and I turned to see what the object was. A gasp left my lungs, and I scurried back as far as I could from Fangreaper, the athame that Richelle used to almost kill my uncle once.

"What are you doing with that?" My voice had an edge to it I didn't recognize.

"Last resort. Use it... on him."

"Fangreaper only works on witches, Sam," I hissed.

"It will kill anything if you stick it in the right place, Ebony," he hissed back.

Footsteps sounded, and I dashed to grab Fangreaper as quickly as I could. My hand had only wrapped itself around the jeweled hilt when the front door swung open and Merlok stepped in with the carcass of an animal. He noticed that Sam and I were sitting side by side, but he only shrugged and slammed the animal on the table.

"I thought you two might be hungry," he said.

Without another word, he ripped off both of the animal's back legs and tossed us a leg each. Sam turned green and looked like he wanted to puke, and I wasn't far behind.

Merlok opened his mouth and sank his jagged teeth into the flesh and fur of the animal. The ripping sound alone made my stomach churn, but I knew I needed to get out of these bonds.

"Merlok?" I asked, my voice as sweet as I could make it.

He regarded me with blood and bits of raw meat hanging from his mouth. "Yes?" he mumbled.

I tried not to look at his face. "How are my... vermin and I supposed to eat when we still have these bonds in place?"

Merlok smacked his forehead. "Of course! How silly of me." He waved his hand and released us from our bonds, but I still couldn't feel my magic. It was like the house itself was stopping me. I silently sighed. Merlok was staring at me intensely, and my stomach churned as I took in the sight of the severed thigh. I threw a look at Sam and his eyes met mine pleadingly. I had to buy time, so I grabbed the leg with the hand that wasn't gripping the athame and sunk my teeth into the fur. Warm blood hit my lips and I gagged, but it seemed to satisfy Merlok. He went back to eating.

I spit out the blood as quietly as I could and I stood up, trying not to make a sound. Sam struggled to his feet and put a hand on my shoulder, and his message was clear. I passed him Fangreaper, and he tiptoed into the dining room. The sound of animal bones snapping masked Sam's footsteps, and I sent a silent prayer to Hecate that this worked. Merlok must have noticed some movement, because he whirled toward us, but Sam was already in motion. He flung himself at Merlok, knife glinting in the air, and sunk the blade into his neck. Merlok made no other noise save for a gurgling sound before he sank to the ground and didn't move. Sam and I wasted no time in getting the hell out of that house, and away from the glassed-over eyes of our captor.

CHAPTER TWENTY-ONE

ONCE WE WERE A safe distance away, we collapsed onto the forest floor. Sam looked pale, so I went to inspect his head. My body sagged as I realized the cut was superficial, and the blood was only making it look worse.

"You're okay. Just a cut," I told him.

"Great, can we get going then?" he snapped.

I shook my head. Even though light was appearing against the horizon, we needed rest.

"We've been up all night, and that cut may look fine, but you still might have a concussion. Let's get at least a few hours of sleep, and then we'll head out."

"I want this done as soon as possible," Sam said, not meeting my eyes.

"Why, so you don't have to deal with what Merlok said in the house?"

Sam still wouldn't look at me, and that all but confirmed what I was thinking.

"Your anger at me isn't just because of Melissa." It wasn't a question.

A muscle clenched in Sam's jaw, but otherwise he gave no indication that he had even heard me talk.

"Sam... talk to me."

"Why? So you can brush me off like you did last time I tried to tell you how I felt?"

"I didn't brush you off. I said no."

Sam scoffed. "You didn't say much of anything, actually. You didn't have to." He said that last part so quietly I wasn't sure if I had heard him right.

"Would it help if I said I wish I could return your feelings?" I brushed a piece of bloody hair back from his face, and he jerked away from me.

"No. I couldn't compete with Nightshade, anyway."

I laughed. "Nightshade dumped me."

"Yeah, I know."

My smile faded. "How did you know that?"

Sam looked at his fidgeting hands. "Peyton."

"Peyton? Tall, brown hair, piercing eyes. Last name of Levin. That Peyton?"

Sam again wouldn't meet my eyes as he chewed on his lip.

My mouth went dry.

"Don't trust that guy," Sam said. "Please, Ebony. He's bad news."

"So are you."

Sam laughed once without humor. "How did you think we've been getting the info on you and your family? How did you think we got in and out of the castle without alerting the guards when we took you and your mom? It was him. It was all Peyton."

The ground swayed beneath me. "No. That's not true." Peyton was a good guy.

Sam clenched his jaw and his eyes tightened. "He's manipulating you, Ebony. I swear it. Yes, I did those things, but it was thanks to *him*."

I shook my head. "No, you did those things because of your girlfriend. Delilah, right?"

Sam swore. "I was with Delilah to forget about Melissa. And you. But she was with Peyton the whole time. I tried not to let it get to me, but it made me so angry. Angry that yet another *thing* took what I wanted. And they used that against me. They used it against you too, and I am so sorry. When I saw him try to get to you during your trial, I had my suspicions of what he was doing, but I never thought you would have fallen for it. I thought—no, I knew you were smarter than that, so I didn't think to warn you. But I'm warning you now. He's the one who's been feeding us information on everything."

I ran my hands through my hair. "How can I trust you? After everything you've done."

Sam shrugged. "You just have to."

I narrowed my eyes. "I'll think about what you've said. For now, let's get some sleep. I'm beat and you need rest."

I curled up on the hard ground and used my arm as a pillow. Sam did the same, and I vaguely wondered if I should've stayed awake so Sam wouldn't kill me.

The mossy cave I have come to know so well in my visions greeted me as I stared into the eyes of Sythion for the second time.

"You killed my most loyal follower." His voice was devoid of emotion, and I had a feeling he was trying to keep his cool.

I crossed my arms. "You need new followers. That guy was a creep."

Sythion's lips turned up into the ghost of a smile. "I'll have admin look into it. For now, though, let's cut the banter. I will give you one last warning to abandon this... foolish mission. You have caused me nothing but trouble, and I am growing tired of your antics."

I sauntered over to Sythion, a smirk coming to my lips. "See, the fact that you're giving me one last warning means I'm close to something. Something you don't want me to know about. Now I don't know what it is you don't want me to know, but I will find out, and when I do, you and your little seal thing are done."

Sythion's eyes blazed. "Be careful who you make threats to, young one."

"Or what?"

My mom appeared before me. Not an illusion like Richelle was. My mom was in the cave with me and Sythion, flesh and blood. Well, sort of. She was corporeal at least, and her face told me something bad was going to happen if I didn't shut my mouth. I didn't listen.

"So, you're going to what?" I asked. "Make my mommy tell me to stop being mean to you?"

Sythion leaned in close, so close I could smell his breath, and let me tell you, that guy needed a Tic Tac. "No. I'm going to do this."

He snapped his fingers and flames danced around my mom, burning every place they touched. She screamed in agony and when I tried to go to her, Sythion caught my arm.

"I can make your mother feel eternal agony. I can torture her over and over again, and she will feel all of it. And your sweet friend Melissa? I can torture her, too. So I would be *very* careful how you proceed."

I tugged my arm away from Sythion and looked at my mom. Tears welled up in my eyes as I watched her burn for the second time.

"Stop," I whispered.

"What was that?" Sythion asked, his tone condescending.

"I said stop." My voice cracked.

Sythion snapped his fingers again, and the flames, and my mom, were gone.

"I'm glad we had this little chat. I think we're finally understanding each other." Sythion turned away from me.

"I will kill you," I said.

Sythion only chuckled as he vanished.

The sun was high in the sky when I woke. I was sweating and I couldn't breathe. The humidity did nothing for my hair, either. Sythion would pay for everything. So would everyone that had ever crossed me. I would make sure of it. I thought about my vision and everything that had happened. Sythion was scared because I was close to something. But what was I close to? I thought about Merlok and how Sythion said he was his most loyal follower. That had to have meant something, but I couldn't think of what. I needed help.

I shook Sam awake, and he blinked up at me.

"Hey. We've slept for long enough," I said.

Sam noticed my appearance and sat up. "Are you okay?"

I laughed at the leaves clinging to the now dried blood on Sam's cheek. "Yeah, I'm alright. We need to get you cleaned up, though. And there's something I need your help with."

Sam looked at me warily. "What is it?"

I helped him up, and I told him everything that happened in my vision as we went to go look for a water source to clean Sam's head.

"That's..."

Sam didn't finish his thought, but I knew he was thinking the same thing I was. If we ended magic, the people we cared most about would suffer, but if we didn't end magic, more innocent lives would be lost. It was a lose-lose situation.

We found a brook nearby, and I helped Sam clean his face and the wound on his head. Luckily it had already scabbed over, but we still needed to worry about infection. I glimpsed a trout swimming and thought how good it would be to eat something that wasn't covered in fur.

"Where's Fangreaper?" I asked Sam.

"I gave it to you yesterday. Remember?"

"But you're the one that used it to kill Merlok."

I had never heard Sam swear before, but he shouted a string of curse words that left me impressed. "I left it in his neck."

"You mean we have to go back to that place?" I groaned, and I gave him a look that said I wanted to stick Fangreaper in *his* neck.

We backtracked to the house, but made no move to go inside. I could almost hear the bugs slithering across every surface.

"Are you going to open the door?" I asked.

"No, are you?"

"No. Why do I have to do it? You're the one who left the knife in there."

Sam gave an apologetic shrug, and I exhaled as I steeled myself and pushed the door open. The smell hit me first, like rotting meat, and the heat and humidity only made it that much worse. And then there were the bugs. More of them had appeared since we left only a few hours ago, and they crawled over every surface, and me. A shiver went down my spine as I shook them off to the best of my ability, but my stomach wasn't having it. I ran to the corner and dry heaved. When I was done, I hurried through the living room and stopped short when I hit the kitchen.

Merlok's body was still on the ground, and a thick layer of bugs crawled all over his corpse. My stomach heaved again. Thank Hecate I hadn't eaten anything. I tiptoed slowly over to Merlok and saw Fangreaper sticking out of his throat. My lungs protested as I tried not to breathe, and I snatched the athame, the blade squelching as I pulled it out of Merlok's flesh. I put it in my waistband, and sprinted back out of the house. Sam caught me, but I tore out of his grasp and wildly shook my entire body, getting all the bugs off.

"Ew, ew, ew, ew." I brushed myself off head to toe, making sure no bugs were left.

Sam looked at me with concern flashing in his eyes and when I calmed down, I gave him what I hoped was a reassuring smile.

"Did you get it?" Sam asked.

I pulled Fangreaper out of my waistband and handed it to him. "I'm trusting you not to kill me with this."

Sam gave me a mock salute and put Fangreaper away. We were about to head back into the forest when I spotted a well-worn path leading away from the back of the house. I tapped Sam's shoulder and pointed and together we went to see where it led.

CHAPTER TWENTY-TWO

THE PATH LED DEEP into the woods and the sun barely made it through the canopy of trees. We walked as far as we could without light and then we lost the trail.

"Wish we had a flashlight," Sam muttered.

"We have my magic, if you're okay with that."

Sam motioned for me to go ahead, and I flicked my hand upward. A ball of light appeared and bobbed ahead of us as we rapidly found the trail again.

"How far does this thing go?" I asked.

"I think we're coming to the end of the trail." Sam said, a sheen of sweat covering his face.

He was right. Water bubbled in the distance. The trail had to end soon. When we finally broke through the trees, the sun was setting below the horizon. We stopped for the night and found a campsite near the trail. Neither of us had eaten in about two days, and we were getting deliriously hungry. I even saw Sam licking his lips at a bird earlier. We found a nice open space near a stream and while Sam went to look for firewood, I took Fangreaper and looked for little woodland creatures to practice my knife throwing skills on. When I had failed to catch three squirrels and a rabbit, I tried another tactic. I walked back to the campsite and found Sam building a fire.

"I didn't know you knew how to do that," I said.

"Boy Scouts," he replied. "Always be prepared. Didn't you catch anything?"

I shook my head, and Sam laughed. "I thought not since it took you so long. That's why I thought I would help."

He held up a snare with two squirrels hanging from the end. I had never been more grateful to see anything in my life. I skinned the animals, trying not to think about Merlok's cabin and the fur and raw sinew I had eaten. Sam cooked them and we dug in. After we ate, Sam and I sat in a comfortable silence, each of us staring at the flames.

"We should probably get some sleep," Sam said.

I nodded, but when Sam went to lie down, I grabbed his hand.

"What is it?" he asked.

I bit my lip, wondering if I should say anything, but after our discussion outside of the cabin, Sam deserved the truth.

"I love you. It's not in the same way you love me and I'm so sorry about that, but I can't see my life without you either. These past few months have been... excruciating. You are one of my best friends and I'm sorry that I hurt you. If I could take it all back, I would."

Sam squeezed my hand and face softened into the boy I knew all those months ago. "I'm sorry too. For everything. I know it won't bring your mom back, but if it helps you feel any better, I can't get her screams out of my head. No matter how much I try. It will always be my biggest regret."

"My biggest regret is Melissa," I whispered.

Sam wrapped his arm around my shoulder. "I know, and I shouldn't keep punishing you for that. It wasn't your fault, it just... it hurt too much. I needed someone to blame."

I hugged Sam, and we sat there for what seemed like an eternity, coming to terms with everything the other had done and trying to heal from it.

The next morning, things between me and Sam were different. They weren't fixed, per se, but I could tell we were trying to mend our relationship. After Sam caught a few fish for us for breakfast (I sent a thank you to Hecate that fish didn't have fur), and we had eaten our fill, we started down the trail again. We didn't even walk for half an hour before we reached an enormous sycamore tree blocking our way.

"I don't get it. Something should be here. It can't just be a dead end." I circled the trunk.

"Maybe this was his walking trail?" Sam suggested.

I screamed as I kicked a rock toward the tree, and the trunk shimmered as the rock went straight through it.

"An illusion," I muttered.

"Huh?"

I grabbed Sam's hand and pulled him toward the tree. "Ebony, what are you—"

We walked right through the trunk and stopped in a clearing. Trees of every variety towered over us, their leaves billowing in the soft breeze. Butterflies that I had never seen before fluttered by, and the chirping of the birds was so crisp it sounded like they were right beside us. In front of us was a cave, and I knew the moss that surrounded its entrance.

"This is it."

"What's it?" My face beamed, but Sam looked confused.

"The Seal of Sythion. It's in that cave."

Sam looked toward the cave, and I let go of his hand as I ran for the mouth. Sam followed me, calling for me to stop, but I didn't want to. I had come so far and endured so much to get here. I had just barely reached the entrance to the cave when an invisible wall stopped me in my tracks. What the hell? I tried to go through, and again I hit the wall.

Sam stopped next to me and carefully put his hand through. Nothing stopped him. He walked a few feet forward and turned back to me.

"Why can I walk right in?"

"Why *can't* I walk right in?"

Sam pursed his lips, and his eyes landed on my arm. "Merlok mentioned something about that mark. He called it a curse? Curse for what?"

"It draws demons to me," I explained.

"Maybe that's not all it does," Sam mused. "Maybe it keeps you from entering this place."

I smacked my forehead. Of course. Sythion didn't want me near the Seal, so he made sure I could never get to it.

"So, how do we take this thing off?" I asked.

Sam shrugged as he walked back toward me. "We'll have to find someone who knows about the curse."

"In case you haven't noticed Sam, the only person who knew anything about Sythion is dead. You killed him, and it's not like I can go strolling back into the city. At least not without getting executed."

Sam looked back at the tree we came through. "That path is too well worn for just Merlok to have come through here." He looked back at me. "What did Sythion say about Merlok in your vision again?"

I thought back. "He said I killed his most loyal follower."

"But not his *only* follower."

I beamed and hugged Sam. "You are a genius! So we just need to find another follower of Sythion and get them to remove the curse."

"I doubt it will be that simple, but essentially, yes."

"Let's go then."

We walked back through the tree, planning to return to the campsite, but stopped when we heard footsteps hastily approaching. Sam pulled me into a thick bush, and we waited.

We didn't have to wait long. A middle-aged woman with pale skin and silver hair down to her butt jogged toward the hidden entrance. I looked at Sam, but before he could even react, I jumped out and pinned the woman to the ground.

"Are you a follower of Sythion?" I demanded.

She hissed and Sam came out of the hiding spot with Fangreaper drawn. The woman spotted the blade and her eyes widened. She turned her eyes back on me and gave me a hateful glare.

"You are the ones who killed Merlok." Her voice was like nails on a chalkboard.

"And we'll kill you too if you don't tell us how to remove the mark on my friend's arm." Sam's voice was devoid of emotion, like he was just talking about what to have for dinner instead of threatening someone's life, and I wondered if it was his defense mechanism.

The woman looked at my arm and cackled. "You have angered our master. You will die."

"Nice try, hag." I said, "Now tell me how to remove the curse."

"No."

Sam handed me Fangreaper. "You know what this is, don't you?" I held the tip of the blade against her throat.

She nodded. I smiled viciously.

"I'm going to cut you up bit by bit if you don't tell me how to remove this mark from my arm."

"Do it. I would never betray Sythion."

"Your friend did," Sam said. "Squealed like that beast on his kitchen table about the location of this place. Of course, that was after we cut off a few fingers."

The hag swallowed hard. "I tell you, and you'll let me go?"

"Absolutely," I promised.

She nodded, and I got off her and hauled her up by her arm. "It's a ritual. You will need a crow feather, some wolfsbane and a drop of your blood all mixed in fresh water. Then you will have to say ' *contra maledictionem*' three times, and the mark should disappear."

I hoped Sam would remember all that because I had already forgotten half of what she had said. I let her arm go, and she ran off, back down the trail.

"Nice lie about the fingers," I said.

"Nice venom in your voice." Sam looked at the ground and he whispered, "I hate it."

"That we can do all that so easily now?"

"Yeah."

I took a deep breath and held it for a moment. When I exhaled, some of the tension from our encounter eased. "We had to. This is too important and we're too close to let something like a silly curse stop us."

"Agreed, but how are we going to find all this stuff? Is there any way we can go back to the city and just buy it?"

"From what store? Demons have destroyed most of them, and I don't know what destruction people have caused since we've been here. No, we'll have to get creative. Besides, a crow's feather shouldn't be too hard to find in a forest this size. It's the wolfsbane I'm worried about."

"I'm not." Sam had a smile on his face as he started walking away from me. I ran after Sam, but he skipped, actually skipped, ahead of me until we got back to the campsite.

He led me to the east, the opposite direction I had gone the night before, and stopped when he came to a cluster of bluish-purple flowers. I recognized them as wolfsbane immediately.

"Ta-da!" Sam beamed.

I wrapped him in a tight hug and kissed his cheek. When I pulled back, Sam's cheeks were red. I pulled a couple of stems and we went back to the campsite to figure out how to find a crow's feather.

CHAPTER TWENTY-THREE

WE HAD BEEN SITTING by a rotting log in the thickest part of the forest for about four hours and hadn't seen or heard a single crow.

"Do you think you could like... conjure one?" Sam asked, fanning himself.

I gave him a look that said "don't be ridiculous" and continued scanning the sky for some sign of a crow. When the forest grew dark, we called it a day, and headed back to the campsite.

On the way back, sitting on a low branch of a tall tree, was a beautiful black crow. Its feathers shone in the fading sunlight and it looked at us like it was saying "I've been waiting for you." The only problem was the crow was perched thirty feet in the air. I sighed and stretched my arms.

"What are you doing?" Sam asked.

"What does it look like I'm doing? I'm going to get the crow."

Sam looked up and whistled. "If you can do that, I'll pay you a million bucks."

I rolled my eyes and squared my shoulders. I climbed the tree. Or at least I tried to. The bark bit into my fingers as I tried to get a handhold, but I couldn't find one. I slipped back to the ground, the tree cutting my hands in the process. I winced, but got up and tried again. This time, I found a few knots in the back of the tree and grabbed the lowest one. I hauled myself up and began climbing the massive trunk.

I was about halfway to the lowest branch when the crow cawed and flew off. A string of swear words left my mouth, but I noticed that when it took off, the crow left a feather embedded between the branch and the trunk. I smiled as I climbed the rest of the way and grabbed the feather. Letting out a low whistle, I signaled Sam and showed him the feather in my hand. He gave me a thumbs up.

Now, how was I going to get down?

I told Sam my problem, and he went around the back of the tree and told me if I slipped, he'd catch me. I didn't know if I trusted his word or not, but it wasn't like I had much of a choice, so I carefully put my foot on one of the knots and started climbing down.

I ended up slipping a couple of times, but I caught myself. When I jumped to the ground, however, I noticed the feather in my hand looked a little worse for wear.

"I hope this will still work." I showed Sam the feather.

"Good thing we have a spare if it doesn't." He showed me a black feather in perfect condition.

"Where did you get that?" I asked.

Sam smiled slyly. "On one of the roots. I found it before you went up to get that one."

I clenched my jaw. So, we weren't totally okay with each other then. I wanted to strangle him, not enough to kill him, but I wouldn't have minded knocking him out for a few minutes. We went back to the campsite, and I chugged down a few handfuls of water from the stream. I looked at the water in my hand and groaned as I realized we had nothing to hold fresh water. I told Sam, and he pursed his lips.

"Maybe we could use a leaf or something."

I found a leaf big enough and dipped it in the stream. It wasn't a lot of water, but it would do.

I hoped.

We put the damaged crow feather in the leaf along with a flower from the wolfsbane plant.

"Now we just need a drop of your blood," Sam said.

I looked at my cut-up hands. The wounds had scabbed over, but I peeled one off and blood started pooling again. I tipped my palm over the leaf and a drop of blood dripped into the ritual mixture.

"*Contra maledictionem, contra maledictionem, contra maledictionem.*" I recited.

Nothing happened. The mark was still on my arm.

"Maybe the leaf messed up the ritual," Sam suggested. "It's another organic element that probably wasn't needed. Also, there's not enough water to hold everything."

"When did you become such an expert in magic?"

Sam rolled his eyes. "I'm not. I'm thinking of this more as chemistry. You know, that class you would have failed had you taken it? Science is precise. I'm guessing magic is too."

I clenched my jaw, but let the insult go.

"So, what do we do?" I tossed the leaf, along with everything in it, aside. "We don't have anything else to hold water other than a leaf."

"Hm." Sam looked around and he gave me a mischievous grin when he looked at me. "Your shoe."

"Huh?" I wasn't sure I heard him right.

"Your shoe," he repeated. "We can use that to hold the water, and since it's yours, it won't mess up the ritual. Hopefully."

I pursed my lips. "That's very... innovative. I like it."

I took off my left shoe and dunked it in the stream. I hobbled back to Sam, and he pulled off another wolfsbane flower and gently laid it in the shoe. We then put the perfect crow feather in, and I dripped more blood into the water. I recited the spell again and this time, something definitely happened.

A flash of golden light erupted from my shoe.

The light then swirled around me as if it was going to pick me up and carry me off. Everywhere the light touched, I felt warm. Like my mom gave me some cookies and a big hug. And when the light reached my arm, the mark shimmered away. The warm golden light snaked its way across my arm and disappeared inside the rose on my palm and with one last flash, the world was dark again. That flash of light had blasted away the mark, and I screamed in triumph.

Sam and I had a celebratory dinner of fish and we went to sleep right after, knowing tomorrow would be a big day.

I woke up before the sunrise the next morning. Sam was sleeping peacefully, and the crickets chirped loud and clear. I had forgotten how magical Amethystia could be. After today, though, I wasn't sure what would happen to the realm. Would it simply disappear? I hadn't even thought of the consequences and now it was too late to turn back. A knot formed in my stomach as I looked at my sleeping friend. No, I had to end magic. Melissa and every other person who had been hurt by magic and the demons running amok deserved that.

I needed to clear my head. My shoe had been by the fire drying all night, so I took the other one off and stepped into the rushing water of the stream. The second the water hit my skin was like clarity hitting my brain. This was the right thing to do, and a new resolve filled my body. I stepped out of the water and woke up Sam, who tried to smack me as soon as I shook him awake. I dodged the attack and told him to snatch some breakfast for us because we were leaving at dawn. He groaned but did as I said, and after we had our fill, we were off to go end magic.

We hiked the hidden path once more and stepped through the tree. Something felt off, and I grabbed

Sam's wrist to keep him from going any further. He asked me what was wrong, but I didn't so much as glance toward him. I was staring at the entrance to the cave, where I saw a male figure step out of the shadows. I gasped as Peyton rushed toward me and wrapped me in a big hug.

"I was so worried about you." His voice had a softness to it that I now recognized as fake. "Are you alright? You're not hurt, are you? How did you get back to Amethystia?"

I rigidly stepped out of the hug. I had a part to play here. He didn't know I knew what he did, and I could use that to my advantage. I forced my body to relax and plastered a big smile on my face.

"I had to get back here. I had to know if you and the others were alright. What are you doing here? How did you find this place?"

Sam looked between us, his eyebrows knotted in confusion. I tried to convey to him by giving him a thumbs up behind my back that I was on the same page as him, but I didn't know if it worked.

"With you gone, someone had to step up and find the Seal. I came across Merlok, a known follower of Sythion, and I convinced him to show me the way.

He's actually in the cave now, getting things ready. Come on, we can go meet him and end things once and for all."

A flat out lie. What was he planning? I played innocent.

"Sam and I were just planning our next move. We found this place this morning by complete accident. That's the cave where the Seal is?" I pointed behind him, knowing full well that's where we were headed.

He nodded and for the first time looked at Sam. "Sam, it's good to finally meet you. I know you and Ebony have had your differences, but she never gave up on you, and I think that shows what kind of friend you are."

Peyton held out his hand in greeting, but Sam refused to take it. Peyton licked his lips and gradually let his hand fall back to his side.

"Anyway, we should get going. I don't know how much time we'll have before Sythion realizes what we're doing."

He turned his back to me, and that's when I moved. I grabbed Fangreaper from Sam's belt and thrust it toward Peyton's back. He whirled on me before I could get a hit and grabbed my wrist. The look of utter surprise turned into a sneer.

"It seems we could never trust you on either side, Sam. What will you do now that you have no one?"

"He has me." I sneered back.

"And you're something to be proud of? By Hecate, it was so hard being around you, Ebony. All you did was whine. Why did Nightshade dump me? Why did Sam have to kill my mommy? It was sickening."

I pushed Fangreaper closer, but Peyton was stronger. He twisted my wrist, and the athame fell from my hand.

"You're the one who's sickening," Sam said with disgust.

The fact that Sam was defending me made my heart swell.

Peyton laughed. "And yet, you're the one who killed all those innocent people."

"Who's really in that cave?" I asked.

"Want to find out?" Peyton whistled twice, and a moment later, Delilah skipped out of the shadow of the cave, sucking on a lollipop.

"Ebony, I'd say it's good to see you again, but that would be a lie."

"Drop the cutesy act, please. It's more sickening than Ebony's whining." Peyton said.

"My pleasure."

Delilah's form shifted and grew taller, more muscular. Her blonde hair shortened and when the transformation was complete, Sam and I both gasped. Because instead of Delilah, Fabian Delacroix stood in front of us.

CHAPTER TWENTY-FOUR

I HAD IMAGINED SEVERAL scenarios in my head where Fabian was still alive, but I had never imagined this.

"I killed you," I said.

Fabian sneered. "It should have killed me when you pushed me off that tower, but I'm a lot stronger than you give me credit for. I broke several bones and was knocked out on the fall down. Peyton here found me before I could drown and nursed me back to health, and then we plotted my revenge."

"So all this time you were..." Sam looked like he would be sick.

"Manipulating you into doing what I wanted? Yes. It was fun. I made myself look similar to... oh, what's the girl's name? The one that I killed. You know her. Anyway...," He turned to me. "I can't let you near that well. See, the one thing dear Peyton didn't tell any of you about the Seal is... it guards a wishing well. Destroying the Seal is not what ends magic, but making a wish through the well will, and it only grants one wish."

The ground was spinning beneath me, and Sam looked like it was doing the same for him. I tried to steady myself as much as I could, but I was feeling the air leave my lungs. I was going to pass out. Sam grabbed my hand and steadied me while I was trying to think of ways out of this. I knew of only one..

"I challenge you. To a duel." My voice was uneven.

Fabian laughed. "I'm not going to take that bait, Ebony. You're a lot stronger than you were several months ago, and even with the way you look right now, I know I can't beat you one on one."

"Then fight me," Sam said, his voice even and strong.

Fabian laughed so hard he cried. "You? You can't be serious. I would snap you like a twig. Of course, that might be fun, so come at me, Sammy."

Sam's face turned red, and his fists clenched at his sides. I wondered if that's what Delilah had called Sam to get him to do all those awful things. I heard footsteps behind me and I whirled around. When I saw Evan coming through the hidden passage, I actually passed out.

My head spun as the world came back into focus. I noticed the earthy smell of the moss first. I opened my eyes, and I was in the cave that held the Seal of Sythion. Not in my visions this time. This time, it was the real deal. The golden seal glowed dimly, illuminating the cave enough for me to see. Sam was bound and gagged in the corner opposite me. I couldn't get to him if I tried, because Peyton, Evan, and Fabian were all crowded around the well, arguing.

"I told you to bring her!" Fabian yelled.

"The little blonde thing was annoying me. I *had* to shut her up." Evan picked at his nails.

Blonde thing? Oh, no. Valerie.

"Still, we needed her alive. You shouldn't have killed her." Peyton was apparently the voice of reason in the trio.

Evan sighed while Fabian paced back and forth.

"No matter." Fabian glanced at Sam with a cruel glint in his eyes. "We have a backup."

Fabian marched over to Sam and hauled him up by his hair. Sam screamed, and I went to save him, only to find myself bound as well. I didn't have a gag, though. Probably so Fabian could hear my screams unfiltered.

"What are you doing?" I shouted.

Evan turned toward me. "Oh, so the princess is finally awake. Good. You'll get to see your demise firsthand."

I scowled. "I always thought you were scum, Evan, and now you've proven me right."

He knelt in front of me. "You didn't think I was scum when we were kissing under the stars years ago."

"And now the memory makes me want to puke."

Peyton snickered. "Don't worry Evan, I bet the memory of kissing me makes her want to hurl, too. Although I will admit, she was one hell of a kiss."

"I swear I will smack that look off your face, Peyton." I sneered.

"You're all talk," Evan said as he strutted back to the Seal. "That's all you've ever been."

I struggled against my bonds, but they held fast. My breath started coming in shallow waves until someone grabbed my hand from behind. I almost yelped, but Nightshade whispered for me to keep quiet. I sagged with relief as he cut through the rope binding me.

"Pretend you are still tied up and follow my lead," he whispered.

I nodded, grateful he was here. I needed to apologize to him, beg him for forgiveness, but for now, we had a job to do. Evan, Peyton, and Fabian surrounded the Seal, and Fabian pushed Sam against the well's edge.

"You know, I'm not sure just a drop of blood will do, boys." Fabian pulled out a dagger and pressed it to Sam's throat. "What do you think, Ebony? Should we spill all his blood?"

Before I could respond with a blast of magic to the face, Nightshade let out a battle cry and heaved his sword toward Peyton. The trio burst into action and scattered as Nightshade's sword hit the stone edge of the well. Sam fell to the ground and scooted toward me as fast as he could while I took that as my cue and jumped up and hit Fabian with a blast of pure magic.

"She really can cast without spells," Evan commented.

"Yeah, I can." I hurled a ball of crackling electricity toward him.

He rolled to the side, dodging the attack, and threw one of his own by shouting, "*Magicae!*"

He wasn't aiming at me, though. Instead, the sphere of magic headed straight for Sam. On instinct, I flicked my wrist, and the attack swerved to the left, hitting the mossy wall of the cave. I looked at my hand as if it was a foreign object and then curled it into a fist. I liked these new abilities. An idea came to me, and I punched the air. A wave of wind shot from my curled fingers and blasted Evan, Peyton, and Fabian against the wall. They slumped to the ground like rag dolls and were slow to get up.

I strolled toward them. All three would pay for what they had done to me and everyone else.

I squatted in front of them, smiling like a cat cornering its prey. "You guys are so dead."

Fabian smiled back, and blood shone on his teeth. "It wouldn't be the first time."

I frowned and trailed my finger down my face, acting like it was a tear.

I was basking in the glory of my victory so much I didn't notice Peyton had his dagger in his hand until it was too late. He hurled the knife, and time seemed to slow as it hit Nightshade directly in the chest.

"No!" I rushed toward him.

He hit the ground as I reached him, and I pulled him into my lap.

"No, no, no, no." I grasped the knife embedded in his skin, wanting to pull it out and inspect the damage, but Nightshade stopped me.

"It will... make me bleed out faster if you pull it out."

Tears rolled down my cheeks and I sniffled.

"I'm sorry," I whispered.

Nightshade weakly wiped away my tears and shushed me. "There is nothing to be sorry for, my love. I am the one who is sorry. I should have never left."

"And I should have been more appreciative of you."

Nightshade smoothed my hair down. "There will… be time later… to reconcile."

We both knew there wouldn't be. "I love you."

Nightshade smiled. "I love you too."

His face went blank, and my world shattered into a million pieces.

CHAPTER TWENTY-FIVE

I SOBBED AS I closed Nightshade's eyes and laid his head tenderly on the stone. I lurched to my feet and balled my hands into fists.

"I tried to warn you," Fabian said, his leg twisted at an odd angle. "I told you to stay out of my way, and you didn't listen."

With a snap of my fingers, Fabian's mouth slowly sewed itself shut. His screams of agony echoed throughout the cave, and I didn't even try to drown them out. I reveled in the sound. Evan, Peyton, and Sam all gaped at me with horror. Sam's face was white, but he said nothing. Evan and Peyton both had sweat pouring down their faces, but I paid them no mind.

I stood in front of the well, and for the first time, actually saw the Seal of Sythion. It was gorgeous with the pentagram in the middle shining like a gold encrusted thread. I hovered my hand over the seal and felt its power rumble through me. If I only touched it...

"Don't, child." Mave appeared in the cave's mouth, along with Aunt Jasmine and Uncle Hesperus. "It's trying to enthrall you. Don't let it."

"It's so pretty." My voice sounded like it was underwater.

"She's right, Ebony." Aunt Jasmine put her hand on my shoulder.

I didn't even notice she had walked up to me, and when she saw Nightshade lying on the cold, hard ground, tears shone in her eyes. She looked at me, the grief making her look older, and less carefree than she used to be, and I shook my head. If I thought about Nightshade for one moment, I would probably do something I would regret to the trio still slumped against the wall.

I held out my hand in a silent command, and Sam approached me. "What is it?"

"I need your blood." I didn't bother to look at him.

"How much?"

When I peered toward him, he had an aura of gold surrounding him so bright I nearly had to squint. The golden aura was guiding me, begging me to kill Sam. It made my rage boil like never before, and I knew I had to listen. More than that, I wanted to listen.

"All of it." I closed my hand into a fist and Sam started choking. Blood started spurting out of his mouth, and he fell to his knees as Aunt Jasmine and Uncle Hesperus rushed to him.

"Stop Ebony," Uncle Hesperus commanded.

I didn't stop.

Mave shook my shoulders. "Fight this child. It's Sythion's influence. He's trying to take away the only variable you need. Don't let him win."

I heard her voice, but it didn't register. Something ethereal clouded my thoughts. Something old. I blinked a couple of times as I realized I was hearing Sythion in the back of my mind. I tried to shake him off.

"That's it, dear." Mave's voice was calm, like she was soothing a child. "Clear your head. Your thoughts are your own and no one else can control them."

The aura around Sam flickered, and I thought I could see Melissa standing behind him with a worried look on her face. The image washed over me like a bucket of ice water. I urgently dropped my hand and Sam started gasping for air.

"I'm sorry," I said. "I didn't mean to—It wasn't..."

There were no words. I had almost killed Sam. Even after everything he's done, he didn't deserve that.

"It's...okay," he choked out.

I helped him to his feet, and he shakily leaned against the well.

"This thing really does mess with people," Sam gasped. "It needs to be shut down."

I held out my hand again, and Sam hesitantly placed his fingers in mine. "It will be. But I need to know you trust me."

Sam's eyes held a wariness to them I completely understood, but he nodded, and I took Fangreaper out of Sam's waistband. I turned his palm over and sliced the blade quickly through his skin. Red appeared instantaneously, and I guided his hand over the seal. At first nothing happened, and I thought I would need to say a spell, but after a few seconds the Pentagram began dissolving wherever Sam's blood touched it. Once the seal completely dissolved we were left staring into a deep abyss.

"What happens now?" Aunt Jasmine asked.

"You make a wish," Peyton said in a mocking tone.

I scowled at him. "Shut up. I'll deal with you later."

I turned back to the well and paused. I glanced at Nightshade's body.

"You could wish him back to life, you know," Peyton said. "Then you two would have all the time you want to reconcile."

Tears welled up in my eyes. I didn't want to lose Nightshade. I couldn't. Then I glanced at Sam. His face told me he knew what I was thinking.

"Don't," he warned.

"You could bring that girl back, too. Melissa, right? Or your mom. You can only choose one, but you could bring one of the people you care about back."

I wanted so badly to believe Peyton. That I could see the people I loved again. Sam put his bleeding hand over mine and shook his head.

"Even if we brought one of them back, what would that accomplish? Everyone would still live in fear and people would still die. It isn't worth it."

"Not even for Melissa?" I asked.

Sam paused and bit his lip. He squeezed my hand and looked me dead in the eye.

"Not even for Melissa."

I took a deep breath and looked down into the vast darkness of the well. The magic deep inside called to me. I opened my mouth, but Fabian tackled me to the ground. He pulled my hair back, and I howled in pain. Aunt Jasmine and Uncle Hesperus tried to pull him off of me, and Peyton scrambled for the well. Sam tackled him, but Peyton didn't so much as budge. Mave waved her hand, and Peyton and Fabian went flying again, this time hitting the back of the cave so hard they lost consciousness.

My whole body trembled as I stood up and glared at them lying there. I made a motion with my hand and Fabian's neck snapped. Evan, still leaning against the wall, pleaded with me, but I didn't hear what he was saying. The three of them took the most important thing away from me, and with another wave of my hand, Peyton's breathing, and Evan's pathetic pleas stopped for good.

I glanced at Sam, who wisely, stayed silent. "Thanks."

I rubbed the back of my head. Sam rubbed his shoulder like he had hurt it when tackling Peyton. I wasn't surprised. Even though Sam had gained muscle in the last few months, he was still lean, and Peyton was much stronger.

I limped back to well and looked into the abyss again. I knew the wish I had to make.

With one last glance at Nightshade, I said, "I wish all magic be ended. Forever."

"No."

Sythion appeared out of nowhere and strode toward us with a scowl on his face.

"What do you mean 'no'?" I scoffed. "I beat you."

Sythion smiled cruelly. "You may have beaten my tests, but you have not beaten me. Therefore, no."

I strode up to him and pointed my finger directly in front of his raggedy face. "Fine then. A duel. You and me. No rules."

Sythion studied my face for what seemed like hours, and whatever he saw softened his features. My face scrunched up, and I tilted my head, but before I could react, Mave stalked up beside me.

"Sythion, you coward!" she shouted. "You have stayed hidden in the shadows all this time, and now you expect all of us to just bow to your will? I don't think so."

Sythion pursed his lips. "Perhaps you were right all those years ago, Mave. I should have killed you."

"And now you will pay for not having the guts."

Mave flicked two of her fingers toward the ground and Sythion dropped to his knees, eyes wide.

"Wha—"

"I have learned a thing or two since we last met, Sythion," Mave said.

She dropped to her knees so that they were at eye level. "I've always wanted to look you in the eye before I kill you."

"Mave, don't." Uncle Hesperus marched up behind her and hauled her to her feet. "We still need him. If you do this, there's no telling what will happen."

A whisper drew me to the well, and I shuffled over, leaving Mave and Sythion to their bickering. I looked down into the dark, bottomless pit, and it seemed to be telling me something, but I didn't know what. I glanced toward Sythion, who now had his eyes downcast, and was murmuring some words too quiet for me to hear. Aunt Jasmine took Mave's place in front of Sythion and had him repeat the words. She got up, walked to me and whispered the phrase into my ear. A spell.

"Why?"

"Mave is right," he said. "I am a coward. That's why I cursed her. I was afraid that if she and my great-great-grandson ever got involved, magic would never be the same, and I knew she would kill me if I didn't scare her into thinking I was more powerful than she was."

"But you created magic, and this world. You are the most powerful being ever," I said.

If he was afraid of what magic would do, maybe I was doing the right thing by ending it.

Sythion smiled sadly.

"No. I'm not. I'm a scientist. Or was. Magic was never supposed to become what it has. It was supposed to be used for the exploration of the universe. To find answers to questions unasked, but I got greedy. The power went to my head, and I thought of myself as a god. When the Delacroix family came into power, I started to realize that maybe magic, the magic I had created anyway, had taken on a life of its own. And then you, Ebony Amberwood, were born. A mixture of two of the most powerful bloodlines, the most powerful of us all, and I knew the day you came into this world what I had done. This wonderful thing that I had created went far beyond what I had meant it to. I tried to scare you into submission, tried to reign in what magic I could, because if I had created it, then surely, I could stop what it has grown into. But you were too stubborn, just like your ancestors before you, and now I am exhausted from trying. The spell will activate the well so you can make your wish. End this chaos, Ebony. For all our sakes."

I tried to imagine what it would have been like, living all those centuries with the guilt that something that was created to be good, could also be used for evil. It would have killed me.

I slowly strode to Sythion and offered him my hand. He took it gratefully, and I smiled at him as I helped him off the ground.

"You aren't that bad for an old man," I said.

Sythion returned my smile. "And you aren't that bad either, Ebony."

I let go of Sythion's hand and took a deep breath as I stared into the depths of the well once more.

I closed my eyes and muttered, "*Da votum.*"

The power of the well shot through me and I held the edge of the well to keep my balance. "I wish to end all magic. Forever."

The cave rumbled and a dim light shone from deep within the well. The light got brighter, and as it got brighter, it was also getting... closer.

"Get back!" I yelled.

Everyone stumbled back, and the light shot out of the well, bursting a hole in the cave ceiling. Rocks and rubble rained down.

Aunt Jasmine grabbed my arm. "We have to go!"

I nodded and started running for the entrance when Nightshade's lavender hair shone in the light.

"No, I have to get him." I turned and started toward Nightshade, but Aunt Jasmine pulled me back. "There's no time. I'm sorry, Ebony, but we have to leave. Now."

"I can't leave him!" I pulled against Aunt Jasmine, but Sam was there tugging on my other arm and together, they hauled me out of the cave. Tears rolled down my cheeks as I screamed for them to let me get him. They didn't listen. We exited the cave just in time to see it crumble down, but the light was still going strong.

Aunt Jasmine shook my shoulders and tried to get my attention. "Ebony, we have to go back to the human world. We have no idea what will happen if we stay here."

I nodded numbly and let her lead me over to where Uncle Hesperus had already opened a portal. We stepped through, just as the light from the well faded and magic was gone forever.

CHAPTER TWENTY-SIX

WE ENDED UP IN the middle of a field. But we weren't the only ones there. Every witch living in Amethystia had landed in the field with us. Some of them looked lost, but most of them looked dazed and confused. One such woman with electric blue hair walked up to me. I recognized her as someone who was in the crowd at my trial.

"Excuse me, miss, are you alright? You look like you're having a rough time of it."

I nodded, not really registering what she had said. She smiled at me and walked away, hugging a man who must have been her husband.

"What's going on?" Sam whispered.

I focused and took in the crowd for the first time. They were all witches, but they all seemed fine with being in the human world. In fact, the only thing they seemed to be confused about was that they were all in a field, and not in their homes. Wherever their homes were. I wiped my cheeks and went over to Uncle Hesperus, who was chatting with my dad. I ran up and hugged Dad until he pushed me away.

"I'm sorry. Who are you?"

I stopped breathing. "Dad, it's me. Ebony."

"I'm sorry. As far as I know, I don't have any kids. You must be mistaking me for someone else."

Dad walked away, and Uncle Hesperus looked thoughtful.

"What's going on? Why doesn't Dad remember me?" I asked.

"It seems... like everyone has forgotten that they were witches. And therefore, have forgotten us."

"But we still remember everything," I said.

Uncle Hesperus nodded faintly. "I don't know why."

"It's because we were at the epicenter of it all," Mave said. "We still have our magic as well."

To demonstrate, Mave waved her hand, and a faint breeze blew through the trees.

"I don't understand. I wished magic to be gone. *All* magic."

Mave shrugged. "Like I said, we were at the epicenter. As far as any of these other fine folks know, they are and have always been human."

I gasped. "What about your curse? Does that mean..."

"My curse has been lifted. I can feel myself aging again. My guess is whatever that light was, it destroyed Sythion along with all the magic."

"And Amethystia?" Sam asked, walking up to us.

"Gone."

Sam took the deepest breath I had ever seen. Almost like he hadn't really been able to breathe since Melissa died.

I gave him a hug, and he squeezed me back. "You don't still hate me, right?" I asked.

Sam shook his head. "I never hated you."

We broke the hug and smiled at each other, and a small spike of happiness ran through me. I kissed his cheek and turned toward my family. "Let's go home."

"Wait, we're forgetting something," Aunt Jasmine dragged her hands through her hair.

"What is it?" Uncle Hesperus asked.

"My house is gone."

"We could use a cleaning spell," I suggested.

"No."

I stuck my tongue out at her. She smiled sweetly back at me.

"We can use Melissa's house," Sam said.

"What?"

He looked at me and his eyes were softer than I had seen them in a very long time. "She wouldn't mind."

"How do you know?" Uncle Hesperus asked.

"Because she told me."

"When she was standing behind you in the cave." It wasn't a question.

Sam nodded. So, I really saw Melissa, and it wasn't a vision this time.

I looked at the sky, clear and blue, with no demons flying around. I had done the right thing. But Dad and Nightshade. My smile faded as a single tear rolled down my cheek.

"It will be okay." Sam squeezed my shoulder. "They're here with us. Always."

I looped my arm through his as we made our way to Melissa's house to clean it up.

"Always."

The next few months were filled with cleaning up the human world to the best of our ability. Demons had hit Salem the worst, but other towns and cities suffered demon attacks, too. Uncle Hesperus took charge of the cleanup duty and Aunt Jasmine helped him from time to time. Mave took a small house by the ocean, and she still regularly came by and helped us with renovations to the house. Sam and I opened a coffee-slash-magic shop where Presto Espresso used to be since the owner unfortunately died in a demon attack. We had so many customers, all wanting readings from me as well as Sam's specialty brew. He called it the McFadden Meltdown because of how much chocolate there was in it. When we weren't at the shop, Sam was helping to rebuild the school and tutor any children and teenagers that needed help, and I was helping to renovate the town.

Sam and I returned home from the shop one day and I collapsed on the couch as he went to the kitchen to make a sandwich.

"White or wheat?" he called.

"White."

He came back with two ham and Swiss sandwiches and set them on the table.

"I want to talk to you about something."

"Okay." I crossed my legs and gave him my full attention. "What's up?"

Sam took a deep breath. "You know how a couple months ago, when we were all in that field?"

I nodded.

"Well, when I said Melissa said we could use the house, she didn't say that in the cave."

"Okay, when did she say it?"

Sam fidgeted with his hands. "When we were in the field."

My back straightened. "What do you mean?"

Sam bit his lip and ran his hand through his hair. "I mean, I've been seeing Melissa wherever I go since that day, and I can't stop seeing her."

I stopped breathing. "Like... like a ghost?"

Sam nodded. "She's not malicious or anything. She's still Melissa, but I thought you should know."

I held out my hand. "I want to see her."

Sam smiled and put his hand in mine. I closed my fingers around his. A faint light glowed in between our palms, and to my right, Melissa slowly materialized.

I stopped breathing for a minute. "Melissa?"

She waggled her fingers in a wave. "Hey, Ebony."

"You can touch her too," Sam said.

I got off the couch and ran my fingers down Melissa's arm. She was fully corporeal.

"Can anyone else see her?"

Sam shook his head. "Just us."

Tears of joy ran down my face as I hugged my best friend for the first time in almost a year. She hugged me back just as fiercely.

"So, when do I get to help out at the shop?" she asked.

We all laughed and for the first time since coming to Salem all those months ago, I felt truly home.

Rate and Review On Amazon and Goodreads

Scan For
Of War and Magic
Playlist

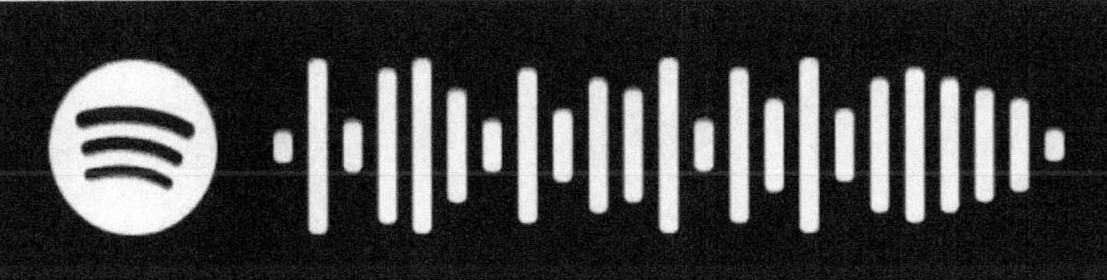

ACKNOWLEDGEMENTS

This book would not have even been possible without the support (both moral and financial) of my amazing mom. She has been my number one cheerleader throughout the entire process of not only creating this book, but creating my author career. She has read my first book more than I have, and I am so grateful for her. Next I want to thank my amazing friends, who are more like family to me. First is Cal who has helped me through breakdowns and who we have spent many, many late nights working on our preferred art forms. Next is Kristin, and while she may be across an ocean, she has been the biggest support of all. She has seen me at my best and worst through this entire process, and I couldn't ask for a better friend. I also want to thank my amazing therapist, McKenna, for teaching me to have grace and self compassion when the hard days arise. She has been part of my support system since the very first mention of me wanting to publish a book. Last of all, I want to thank you, my readers, because without all of you, I would not be doing what I am. You guys have made my dream of being an author come true and I couldn't be more thankful.

ABOUT ME

Julie Caldwell was born and raised in Oklahoma where she still resides with her little black cat Absynthe. Julie fell in love with reading when she was very little when her mother would read stories to her at bedtime. Her love of reading quickly translated into her love of writing, first with poems, and then with full length novels. She has a love of anything mythological or having to do with the occult. Her hobbies include playing video games, and photography.